THE EMPTY DANGER

Volume 1 of

The Book of Exquisite Corpse

Anna Tizard

Deeply Weird
P R E S S

The Book of Exquisite Corpse

THE EMPTY
DANGER

Anna Tizard

Foreword

On Exquisite Corpse

I discovered the game of Exquisite Corpse several years ago when I was working in a call centre. If you have ever worked in a call centre you may have experienced the same kind of brain-itching frustration, from dealing with the same enquiries over and over. Your mind begins to feel parched. The computer screen seems like a box in which your thoughts must be contained, so you find yourself, whenever you get a whiff of a break, seeking out the most bizarre conversations you can manage, if only to prove you're still capable of thinking something different, something else.

But there's another side to call centres which may make you stay longer than you promised yourself you would. The most interesting and diverse people can be found working in these often transient roles: people with second jobs, unusual careers or aspirations that take time to get off the ground. People just like me, and yet wonderfully different. In our team I met a local DJ; an actor; a bloke with a degree in a very specific type of engineering, waiting for a very specific job offer to crop up in the newspaper (I think it took 2 years in the end); and someone who wanted to start their own pub.

We got on brilliantly, but for me, chatting wasn't enough. In between calls I started up a game of Consequences, the old parlour game where you each write a particular part of a story, cover up your answer and pass it on to the next person who, not seeing what you've written, writes the next bit. With people taking calls at different times, we inevitably got into a muddle about who was writing which part when, so for a while we gave up on the rules and wrote freestyle, leaving just our last sentence visible to the next person. This proved to be both baffling and hilarious, and I seem to remember a story about a caged monkey fight that made no sense whatsoever, but was nonetheless deeply pleasing.

It was a French-Spanish colleague who pointed out that Consequences was also known in France as Exquisite Corpse. Thrilled by the bizarreness of this title, I looked it up and was immediately hooked by the origins of this confusion: in the 1920s, the French Surrealists crystallised the original story-building game so that the purpose of each round was to produce a single sentence, with incredibly weird results. Roughly translated, the group's first attempt was: "The exquisite corpse shall drink the new wine".

This was it. This was our new game.

We played with a delicious new intensity, our imaginations sparking off each other like fireworks foolishly shoved inside the same cardboard box. But sneaking slips of paper to each other under our manager's keen surveillance had its own dangers – like being overcome by laughter and sliding helplessly off your chair onto the floor. (Yes, that was me.) So we made a pact to explore the game properly, no holds barred, after work in the local pub.

The wonky wooden table was only just big enough for the six of us to play, with our drinks clustered in the middle. I doled out a handful of game slips I'd printed which detailed the different types of words needed at each turn (e.g. adjective, noun, adverb and so on. Please see my "How To Play" page at annatizard.com for a complete guide as well as said game slips). As we scribbled, the pressure of giggles grew, threatening to break through the bubble of our studious silence.

At the end of each round we took turns to read out the sentences we'd created. Sometimes we were laughing too much to speak, which of course only made it funnier. Other times we were struck with wonder at the synchronicities that occurred: words and themes we'd chosen independently but which went hand in hand with each other, or seemed to describe each other's recent experiences. Were our minds connecting in some way that went beyond words?

By the end of the session we had chuckled and gasped our way through nearly fifty rounds (of Exquisite Corpse, not drinks!) for a non-stop two hours. What drew the event to a close was the lateness of the hour, the simple need to go home and eat. As we shrugged on our coats, I gathered up the crinkled slips of paper: precious tickets to a deeply weird zone of thinking.

Now, several years after that first session and many others since, I find myself still poring over those bizarre sentences I meticulously typed up afterwards. I'd known by instinct that they were meant for something more: a strange magic, to stow away for a rainy day.

And now it rains. Puddles open their eyes to the sky. Those mismatched words whisper hints of inspiration, an otherworldly sensibility that beats behind everyday details. What began as a silly game has led to a deluge of stories; dark, occasionally humorous, and always unexpected. Each one was born of these mysterious mind connections; perhaps that's why so many of them are haunted by that very possibility.

Won't you join me? Leave your umbrella at the door.

The Empty Danger: When a round of Exquisite Corpse produced that eerie word combination, the question of "What could that be?" had me transfixed. Was it a danger that happened to be empty (in what way?) or was it the emptiness of the thing that rendered it dangerous? How could something that was intangible pose a real, physical threat?

The mostly likely answer seemed to be: "fear". Fear is an abstract concept yet it inspires in us an actual chemical reaction in our brains and nervous systems. It makes us think and *behave* differently, and so what begins as an idea or a thought enters the realm of the physical. At first I dabbled with a few ideas as to how to turn this into a story, but none of them took – until March 2020. That is when fear began to take on a new meaning and a new power for me.

In the UK, the coronavirus pandemic was gaining momentum, as it still is at the time of writing. The prospect of a national lockdown went from unthinkable to a legal requirement within a period of two weeks. Throughout it all, my sense of disbelief was coupled with an awareness of a rising potent force, a collective energy: the unknown, the impossible, had entered our midst and life was not the same. The threat was invisible and airborne, carried by people who had no symptoms. In the office where I worked, the air itself seemed to thicken as if clotting with our anxiety, hanging low and heavy like dense clouds over our desks. I say "our" anxiety because it was clear that everyone was thinking and feeling the same things.

If this cruel situation has taught us anything about ourselves, it is that we are all inextricably connected. What we think and what we do affects others. We are all in this fear-soup together, and together we face it.

I wrote *The Empty Danger* partly to try and get a hold on my own fear, and the grief that still sometimes sweeps over me when I watch the news. It hurts even to lose strangers. But there is hope to be found in this newfound shared-ness, this empathetic fog so many of us live in. On the flipside of all the pain and loss, it demonstrates that we are capable of doing so much to help each other. Even – perhaps – just by choosing to think in a particular way.

Anna Tizard, 20th September 2020

Part 1

The Trespass

I stood on the kerb and pressed my phone closer against my ear so the wind wouldn't catch on the receiver.

"Sorry, what was that?"

It was weird enough that Clare, the manager of the finance team, was calling me after work, but I couldn't process what she'd just said.

She repeated herself. "Jake, who led our training session today, has developed symptoms of the coronavirus."

I felt none of the usual irritation at hearing Clare's voice. Instead, something like a piece of ice slithered into my stomach where it pooled and grew nauseous.

No. No.

"But he looked fine. He seemed fine." My voice sounded distant, like somebody else's.

"It was towards the end of the day when he started to feel unwell. He just called us to let us know."

A car murmured past, such an ordinary sound. The road was clear. I was waiting to cross, but I stayed where I was, bracing my free arm across my front against the cold wind, repeating Clare's words in my head, but all the meanings were jumbled.

"He's going to be tested shortly," she said.

"How long – "

"It takes… about four or five days, I think?"

"Four or five days!"

"We'll all need to self-isolate."

I hesitated. There was still a gap in the traffic. I'd be better off finishing this conversation indoors, in the warm. But I couldn't move. The edge of the kerb dug against the soles of my shoes while I stared at the building opposite: the red bricks, a light on in our flat's window, second floor up. The natty old TV aerial blown sideways on the roof, like a stick man gone wrong, waving its arms in a silent *"Help!"* Another car groaned past, a blur of dull silver in the edge of my vision.

It was pizza night. Sarah would be wandering around in her dressing gown, having showered off the lab smell as soon as she'd got home. Matt and Carlos would be sprawled either end of the sofa, debating how much garlic bread to get. I needed to get inside, dump my stuff and make sure they ordered my pepperoni.

But I was infected. Very likely infected. I was going to be ill, maybe soon, maybe seriously.

I couldn't go home. I'd infect them all. Sarah was my best friend, practically my psychotherapist. The guys... they were decent people; yes, they were friends as well as my flatmates. Why should they suffer because of one man, one meeting? Because of something that had happened to me?

Clare's voice broke through a gathering hurricane of thoughts. "Are you okay? Do you have everything you need?"

Oh no. Clare had shaken his hand. I saw her do it.

A fierce, strange compassion gripped me. I didn't particularly like Clare, but I didn't want her to get ill. Thankfully I didn't have time to blurt out anything stupid: I reacted to her practical question and switched back into work mode, running a finger down my bag's shoulder strap.

"I've got my laptop and my charger on me. I can answer emails..." But most of the systems weren't available off the premises, were they? They always said it was for security reasons – as a financial institution, that sounded right – but I guessed they just didn't want to spend the money on one overarching system that could handle all the different functions and accounts.

"IT are working on a secure virtual gateway so we can access all systems remotely," said Clare. It sounded like a sentence she'd rattled off many times; I could picture her nodding as she said it. "In the meantime, I'm afraid there's not much you can do, other than sit tight. Stay in touch by email, stay isolated as much as you can and… let us know."

The bit she didn't say out loud crashed in my ears, a crest of horror breaking over me. *Let us know…* if and when you get sick?

So that was it.

Somehow, we'd ended the call, wishing each other well. I was still there on the kerb, still waiting to cross.

All that stuff Sarah and I had argued about yesterday. I knew this pandemic was going to get big, out of control. She kept saying I was worrying unnecessarily, that there was no point in stressing about something that might never happen.

Well, she was right about that. No amount of worrying in advance could have prepared me for this.

The road was still clear, like it was mocking me. I stared up at the big window into our lounge. With a long bus commute, I was always the last one in.

I frowned at my phone and scrolled for Sarah's number, then shoved it back in my pocket. I couldn't speak to her yet. I couldn't listen to her plain, sensible logic, not when everything was so wrong. I needed to walk first.

I turned and began hurrying along the pavement. My feet seemed a long way down and yet there they were, doing what they always did, one flashing in front of the other like they knew exactly where I was going. Where was I going?

Just keep moving.

It *couldn't* be a simple case of going straight home and passing the virus on to all of them. Could it? There had to be another option. But I couldn't afford to go and stay in a hotel… And what hotel would let me in, if they knew? I wouldn't deceive a bunch of strangers like that. It was just as bad to pass it on to strangers. Worse, if I didn't tell them. Why should they put themselves at risk for me?

I was infected, wasn't I? I had to be.

I had a flash-forward of what it would be like at home. Staying in my room as much as possible – at least my room was next to the bathroom. Sarah bringing me soups, doing all the food shopping. And I would – what? Sit on my bed day after day, browsing social media, playing Patience and Angry Birds. Would I even get a test? I probably had to go out somewhere to get that: bad idea. I tried to remember what they'd said on the news. Some countries like Germany were doing loads of tests. The UK, not so much.

Damn – if only my parents had listened to me about converting their crumbling garage into a second living room or mini cinema, that would've been perfect...

Logic said it was inevitable I had to go back to the flat, but I wasn't ready to accept that. Not yet. I was stubborn, an idiot, but this didn't feel right. There had to be another way. *Sarah, just let me have my moment of irrationality.*

I pushed on against the chill wind, following the slope of the pavement, tracing the rise and fall of garden walls and fences until they trickled away and were replaced by the wire fence at the end of the park. Did I want to go to the park? Not while it was getting dark. But I needed somewhere to sit and think. A bench, but somewhere quiet.

Suddenly I knew where my feet were taking me. There was only one bench I wanted to sit on, although the thought of it gave me a jolt of sadness. It was like a memory of hope rather than hope itself. I so wanted to have that feeling of hope, lost to me now.

Down curving roads, past houses that seemed faceless now that the light was fading. I'd have to call Sarah soon; she'd be wondering where the hell I was. They might still order my pepperoni, but if I wasn't back when it arrived, Carlos would be tempted to eat it.

"Take it, Carlos," I whispered to the street, then glanced around to see if anyone was listening. No-one. Everyone was home, cosy indoors. But a pair of eyes caught my attention: a tabby cat, curling its tail around the lamppost, mewing for a fuss. I reached down but stopped myself just in time. If I had the virus, I might leave traces in her fur and pass it on to her owners.

I shoved my hands into my jacket pockets and kept walking.

Would the gate be open? Seeing the stone building at last, I rushed the last distance, throwing a cursory glance for oncoming cars while I jogged across the road. It was hard to tear my eyes from the shadow of the big yew tree where the gate would either be open or closed.

Closed – but locked? I nudged up the latch with the crook of my elbow and pushed it open with my foot, holding back a sigh of relief so I wouldn't breathe virus-breath all over its black metal surface.

The garden was empty. I exhaled, but something other than relief welled up inside me. The churchyard looked so small in the light of the mini street lamp. Light bowled softly against the lower branches of the oak tree, making them look like elephants' trunks.

To see the winding path again was to remember the kids running along it, squealing and trying to clamber up the branches when I'd asked them to find some ideas from nature for our next project. Of course, half of them had run straight to the gravestones at the back, their eyes bright with morbid fascination. Was that why we'd ended up making clay gargoyles that time? I couldn't remember how I'd settled on that idea in the end.

This place reminded me of a time when my hopes were big, huge even. Had I really believed it was the beginning of something? That a few freebies for some disadvantaged local kids might lead to fee-paying groups and supplement my non-existent income as an artist selling sculptures and paintings?

As I took in the scene, business ideas still buzzed within me like flies that refused to die, nuzzling against a window that was long shut. I wandered along the thinning path, touching the tops of wildflowers, breathing in the earthy scent. In the crook of a tree trunk an object like a large, twisted stone stood out, shadows leaning from its weird features. I crept closer and took in a breath. A clay gargoyle! Like a ghost of this place, a ghost of the good memories. As I reached for it the little boy who made it sprang into my mind: Kyle. So sweet and quiet. Those deep, dark eyes, serious and hesitant. Yet when he got into modelling there was no stopping him.

I edged closer, spellbound. The grey figurine was squat, hunched, with low hanging wings peeping out either side. Its ugly great mouth stretched open in a grimace; the tongue sloped over its chin. From under the meticulous fur-effect eyebrows, two deep dents stared at me. I had to break a grin. I could actually remember Kyle scooping out the eye holes with the end of a pencil – the same one he'd used to sketch the drawing he'd made first of this fantastic gargoyle, surely the best of the bunch.

My smile dropped. "He left it here. He never took it home with him…"

A twig snapped, and I glanced up, heart thumping.

A pale face emerged from the semi-darkness beyond the trees. I gasped and covered my mouth, immediately embarrassed at having reacted this way. It was only the gardener.

I opened my mouth and raised my hand in a wave, but something was wrong. He looked different. His eyes were distant, like they were fixed on something surrounding me. For an odd second, I had the sensation that I was semi-invisible, that none of this was really real. That the effect of getting the virus – which in any case seemed like something out of a horror-fantasy or sci-fi movie – was to make me less real…

I inwardly tutted. Sarah was always saying, "Don't let your weirdo imagination get the better of you."

The gardener came towards me with those long, loping strides I recognised, an uncertain smile on his lips. "Hello? Can I help you?"

"I'm so sorry. I suppose it is late, isn't it? You *are* Dale, aren't you?"

I smiled, relieved to have finally remembered his name. He had to recognise me, surely. True, it had been nearly two years ago that I'd run the group, but he was often there in the background, quietly digging or pruning. He would wait until the unsuspecting kids came closer, then he would thrill them with monster roars, stomping around with deliberate clumsiness as they scattered in all directions – trampling his flowerbeds, which never bothered him as much as I thought it would.

Dale's features resettled into surprise. "Oh yes! It's you!" His eyes flicked meaningfully to the gargoyle in the tree.

"Elina." I nodded, pinning my arms behind my back against the urge to shake his hand. "Actually, sorry, I've just been told I have to keep my distance…"

"Oh." He glanced away, cheeks darkening. A memory pinpricked my fretful state of mind: Dale had always struck me as a bit childlike. And he always seemed to be here, gardening. I guessed he was trying to work through something, some trauma or mental difficulty. That would be just like Paul, the Pastor, to take someone in like Dale and give them a job. Dale managed a cheerful enough exterior, but sometimes a haunted look floated into his eyes.

Like now. Still holding his spade as he emerged from the shadows.

"It's Paul you'll be after, isn't it?" Dale's eyes hooked on me, appraising. With his free hand he rubbed his unshaven chin. It was so quiet in the garden I could hear the bristles rippling under his rough fingertips.

I frowned. Had I come here to just sit on the bench and think? Or did I want to talk to Paul? Guilt about finishing the kids' group flashed through me; that was probably the reason I hadn't stayed in touch with my old friend. But it was early evening, nearly dark now, and I'd be interrupting his meal.

"Wouldn't it be better – " I began, meaning to suggest I went and knocked on Paul's door a little later, but Dale had set off at a fast march, and I only had time to see him lean his spade against the fence before the gate clanged and he was gone.

I was left alone in that garden, under the weak spot light of the Narnia-style lamp post. It felt like a tiny movie set, which matched my mood exactly: it was surreal. I should be at home by now, tucking into pizza in front of the TV, watching some quiz show or the latest murder series Carlos was trying to get us into. Instead I was here, outdoors, shivering while the tall grasses of the wildflowers shuffled this way and that in the breeze. The artificial light bleached them of colour, turning them into grey ribbons.

How ill was I going to get? How soon? What was I going to do?

I sat down on the bench, cursing myself for touching the wooden seat. Too late. Maybe Paul would have something to clean it with. I needed to get some alcohol gel. I needed a mask.

If I went home, Sarah would take over the whole operation like it was a war effort. She'd shop for everything: plastic gloves, anti-viral sprays for door handles. She'd chivvy the boys into doing their share of cleaning, cheerful military style, perhaps even get a bit Mary Poppins just to annoy them. Matt, for one, could barely be bothered to wash up his own plates. But it was all too logical. I didn't want logic. I wanted something irrational and impossible to come along and magic everything better – to go back in time and not bother to go to work today so I would miss the training session and would never have been exposed. How long was it before I had to accept the inevitable?

Footsteps on the gravel made me stand up.

It was Paul, in his jeans and black polo neck, his big smile.

"Hi, Paul."

"Elina, how are you?"

I realised I was readying myself for a hug and took a step back. "Don't come too close. Sorry. I've just been told I've come into contact with the virus. But I haven't touched anything, except this bench..."

Paul's forehead creased in worry. "I'm sorry to hear that, Elina." His warm voice was a mix of London and faint African accents. A big, cosy, welcoming sort of voice, like a great storyteller. While my stomach churned over the awkwardness of what was to come, it soothed me just to hear him again. Maybe that was all I could expect from this.

Just seeing Paul's face brought a rush of memories rising like tears to my eyes: the kids' group. How sheepish I'd felt those first few times, embarrassed in front of the children; how Paul had coached me, got me to relax with them, saying, "It's not school, and they know it." Autumn afternoons with the low sun streaming through the windows, the busy silence as eight or nine children become completely absorbed in the artwork they were making. Pure magic.

"It's good to see you," he said.

"I'm sorry it's been so long." I wasn't quite ready to tell him everything, though I could feel it coming. My knees felt like putty so I sat on the bench. Paul nodded and settled on a tree stump a short distance away. Patient as ever, he understood straight away that I needed a moment to compose myself, to chat about other things.

"I guess… I felt a bit bad about the way things turned out. I had to go and get a 'normal job' after all." I even hooked my fingers around the inverted commas. Oh God, I'd interrupted Paul's evening, and now I was going to throw a bunch of problems at him that he could likely do nothing about. The least I could do was level with him as quickly as possible.

Every second hammered in my ears. What was wrong with me?

But then it hit me: saying it out loud was like admitting the reality of my situation. Maybe this was the real reason I'd staved off ringing Sarah. I needed to tell someone else first. Someone like Paul, whose job it was to listen and whose personal circumstances weren't potentially ruined by my news.

Paul brooded, his hands loosely clasped together over his lap while my explanation spilled out, broken and stumbling, my mouth parched. It was as if my throat was trying to stop it all coming out.

"My friends. I can't just go back and infect them all. I mean, I could, in fact I don't even think I have any choice, but… it's horrible. I hate this. Not having a choice."

I swallowed, but it was all still there, still close, this poison just sitting in my throat. I'd almost forgotten this quiet way Paul had, of lifting the truth out of you with just a look. Straight out.

He paused. He shifted on the tree stump, as if he had to rethink his instinct to reach out a hand. More changes he might have to make soon, for all his work with people, if this coronavirus thing escalated in the UK.

"OK, first things first. None of this is your fault. I know that's obvious on the conscious level, but your unconscious mind probably has something else to say." He raised an eyebrow. How well he knew me. "And at this point, we don't know for absolute certain that you're infected, do we? How close did you get to this person?"

I sank my cheeks into my hands. "When I think about it, we all touched everything the trainer touched. The coffee dispenser, those handouts. Then there's the door handles. He shook Clare's hand! She must be really freaking out…"

I could feel my breath speeding up, the more I spoke. I stopped and stared at my shoes. It was 'dress down Friday', so I was wearing my trainers. Usually the sight of them made me feel elated, ready for the weekend, but they looked alien to me in the whitish light, drained of colour. Sort of pathetic. They were tipped around the edges with ashy dust from the gravel path.

Paul spoke softly. "Fear is a tough emotion. There's so much of it around at the moment, bubbling under... I'm afraid that your friends are already burdened with this, though they don't yet know it, unless there is some other practical alternative?"

I hesitated, unsure whether he was asking me outright or just thinking aloud, feeling his way around the ideas the way he sometimes did. Well, I wasn't going to interrupt if he had one of those thoughtful, faraway expressions in his eyes – which I couldn't see from here. With his head tipped forward, chin on his hand, the lamp light illuminated his forehead, but his eyes were sunken into the shadowed slope beneath.

I sat clutching the bench, listening to the wind swirling the oak tree's branches, my hair whipping about my face; wondering how long it would be rude not to say anything. Wondering why I expected something like magic to just sprout out of this man's mind.

A soft thump sounded across the garden, lost in darkness. It might have been a twig dropping off the tree and knocking the fence, but Paul's head flicked up, attentive.

"Dale's friend. Feeling a bit nosy, are we?"

A crow barked twice. Surprised, I stared into the darkness at what might have been its beak, just a fleck of shine, before the bird flapped off noisily.

"How did you see that?"

Paul smiled. "I just recognised the sound. They're always hopping in and out – they're quite tame, some of them. Dale spends a lot of time in this garden…" He trailed off, his smile lost in doubt. Fair enough: it was inappropriate for him to say any more. Dale was his effectively his patient.

"I've heard they can use tools," I said. It calmed me, just to consider this simple, easy fact. A completely non-life-and-death matter. *Crows use tools.* I took a deep, slow breath and let it out again, thinking only of that.

Paul nodded. "It's true. Listen, I'm sorry your art company didn't work out for you the way you wanted it to. But you can still try, find another way…"

I blinked at the sudden change of subject, but this was probably one of those counsellor things – to get the person to talk about their life as a whole and hopefully make the immediate problem seem less scary in context.

"Of course, it won't be quite how you envisioned, but you never know how things work out..." He looked at me, his expression gentle. "You had a real connection to those kids, too."

"I know..." My mouth twisted guiltily.

"It's a shame for you, too, I meant. These things have a way of opening us up."

I turned on my seat to look at him. "What do you mean by that?" These big, sweeping always statements frustrated me – but I heard my demanding tone and blushed. I was getting too much into this 'honest' mode. We used to have these friendly meaning-of-life debates while the kids were running around the garden, but here, in the darkness and cold, it felt utterly wrong.

"Sorry, I didn't mean to sound so blunt," I said quickly. "But I do want to understand: what did I open myself up to?" He wasn't talking about his belief system, was he? Paul was well aware I didn't share his, and he'd never pressed the matter. So far.

"Ah. I've missed you, Elina, with all your questions." He chuckled. "The psychologist is back!"

I bit my lip then laughed anyway. "God, it was only an A-level course," I said, then felt bad about saying 'God'.

"Life," said Paul, nodding at me. I didn't understand. Was he correcting my use of the word 'God' to 'life'? Was that the all-holy thing at the centre of it all?

Seeing my confusion, he said, "We open ourselves up to life. This experience, on this plane." He held out his hands to the garden.

Silently I asked, *What other plane might there be?* But this was religious stuff, and you either bought into it or you didn't. It wasn't my territory... for now. I had enough on my plate. An immediate problem I needed to resolve right now.

Okay, so I didn't believe everything he believed, but that didn't mean I couldn't enjoy his company and his problem-solving skills. "So... any ideas what I should do?"

"Stay here." He spread his arms wide again.

I looked around me, at the wildflowers casting striped shadows over each other, the old, lopsided gravestones that I couldn't see, but I knew were there, further back. What did he mean? Sleep on the bench? But – oh no. If he had a spare room, I wasn't going to take it. That was way too much of an imposition. Besides, I'd pass the virus on to *him.*

He watched me carefully. "I meant the church hall. It's not ideal, but if you really want somewhere to stay and keep a social distance from absolutely everyone, I've just cancelled all events until July."

I stared across at the white door which glowed dimly in the edge of the light. The church hall was where we'd held the kids' art group; a modern, oblong extension to the church which looked a bit like an outbuilding.

"But... That's really very generous of you, but... what would I sleep on?" Images of the interior quickened through my mind. The racks of chairs stacked along the wall. Of course, it had a kitchen area! It was small and practically antique, but still. I'd have to cut through to the church to get to the toilets... I couldn't believe I was warming to the idea already, except for the one obvious thing lacking: a bed.

"Perhaps one of your flat mates could drop off your duvet, amongst other things. You should be able to make up a bed using sofa cushions. I seem to remember from my early days roughing it as a young evangelist, if you stuff a few sports bags with enough clothes and line them up, they can be more comfortable than some of the worst mattresses in this world."

I shivered with the delicious weirdness of it. Could this really be happening? Only ten minutes ago I was dizzy with the impossibility of my situation, not really believing there was a way out. The sports bag thing had to be hideously uncomfortable, no matter what he said – how bad could those hotel mattresses be? – but I didn't care. A light had come on inside my head. A feeble but welcome light.

My mind was racing with so many details I hadn't worked out what to say.

"Don't answer me yet," said Paul. "Speak to your friends. I'm sure they'll help you make sense of it. But either way," he added, standing up, "I'd like to think you already have what you came here for."

"What's that?" I stared back dumbly.

"A choice."

Silence stung the phone line. I thought of all the internet lines and wireless phone lines that criss-crossed the air right now, a web of connections being tried and made, conversations going on. Possibly there were many at least as weird as this one.

Sarah repeated it back to me. "You're moving in to the church hall." She was piecing together the words, checking my logic for holes. I sensed she was also holding back a tide of shock and worry. I hadn't given her time to react to the news of my likely infection before I threw this new development at her.

But despite the obvious danger posed to her by my staying at home, she wasn't going to be hurried in to this new idea. "Won't it be cold?"

"Um, there's a heater, I think." Paul had already unlocked the door for me, but for some reason I couldn't bring myself to go in and check these things. I *had* to stay there, it was the only viable choice.

"What about a cooker or hotplate?"

"There's a whole kitchen in there, Sarah. It's bigger than ours! True, it's ancient. But they use it for events and stuff. Remember, I used to do the kids' art group in there." I had a stabbing urge to add, *back when my life had a purpose.* "If I'm using electricity, I guess I'll just have to pay him at the end."

"The end? When is the end?" She half-whispered it to herself.

No way was she going to freak out. That was my job. I ignored the rhetorical question and brought her back to the issue at hand. "I'll stay here until I'm clear of this thing. What is it they say? Ten days after you've had symptoms? Fourteen? I'll look it up. There's no way I'm infecting you."

"You might infect Paul," she said quietly.

"I hope not." I took a moment. "Actually, the chances are pretty low. He has no need to come in to the church hall. He's already cancelled their events. I think he's pre-empted the total lockdown that might happen across the whole country, soon enough."

"It is happening, isn't it?"

"I think so."

Silence again. This wasn't like us. In fact, it was downright topsy-turvy. Sarah was leading on the doubtful silences. I'd rung her *after* I'd worked out a solution. But this was a different type of problem than usual. I wasn't just feeling low for no apparent reason. There was nothing for her to psychoanalyse; she couldn't even offer me a chocolate bonbon with a mug of tea.

It struck me that she might be busy in this silence, trying to find a reason I should come home.

"I'm not coming home." There, I said it. "I have another option, and I'm going to take it."

She laughed once. "I like this new decisive Elina."

I felt a smile widen on my face, but it was stopped by this horrible, creeping feeling underneath my skin.

"I don't like... any of this. Sarah, I'm scared. I've probably got the coronavirus. And I don't know what's going on with my job. The systems, they're not even set up remotely! Not the ones our team uses. Not the band four numpties. They'll get rid of me!"

"They can't just get rid of you..." Sarah's sensible tone was back. I imagined her fisting her hip as she spoke.

"They might. They could make me redundant. If proper lockdown goes ahead, just imagine. Companies everywhere will be losing so much money." I was pacing now, back and forth in front of the bench. I forced myself to stop. "At least... you'll be okay, won't you?" Sarah was a lab technician for a medical company.

"I think so... I don't think we can do lockdown, not properly. We'd lose too many experiments. Besides, we wear so much protective equipment anyway that there's no need to shut us down. I guess – all I have to is don my work gear before I get on the train!"

We laughed. How much I missed this feeling, already. I'd only been gone an hour or so. But everything had changed.

We went through the things she'd need to drop off for me: toothbrush, change of clothes (she could always drop more off in a day or so), duvet. My share of the pizza.

"It'll be all right, you know," she said. "Things'll work out."

Really? How did she know that? How could she be so confident? Or was she just being the counsellor again?

"Remind me, Sarah. Why didn't you take psychology any further? You know you would've made a great counsellor. I'm being serious."

She snorted, still playful. "Because I didn't want to spend all my time talking to people about their problems – oh wait – look, here I am."

"Oh, ha ha..."

"Well, you know. With psychology I was looking for something a bit different, maybe something downright un-sensible before I settled down to a sensible degree in chemistry."

"And did you find it?"

"Well, I met you, didn't I?"

I gasped in mock dismay. "Dr Sarah! That's most unprofessional."

"Yeah, well, where else would I get my entertainment? And no, Matt's quiz show obsession does not constitute entertainment. Thank God for my job…" Her tone changed, and I could hear the frown in her voice. "Oh, sorry."

"S'okay… So. Any other instructions, Dr Sarah?"

"Yes. Just – don't spin out of control, okay? I'm asking you nicely." She hesitated. "Or else I'll get Matt on to you."

I frowned. "What's Matt gonna do? Quiz me to death?"

"Well that's just the thing. You're like the best puzzle ever. Every time I solve you, you go and mess yourself up all over again."

Fifteen minutes later, Matt's car pulled up. Out they both came, struggling up the path with armfuls of sofa cushions. I stood well back as Matt and Sarah sidestepped through the church hall door to drop the pieces of my new bed in a heap against the wall. Their second shift included two bags of my clothes, plus a bag of pasta, jars of sauce, bread, teabags and my favourite raspberry jam. Sarah was still reeling off lists of things she'd buy and bring over tomorrow night, even as they both backed off, waving, towards the car.

And so I was alone. The lamp's light seemed colder than ever, bleaching the grass of its green before the rest plunged into blackness. I was grateful for having one last conversation before turning in, although the idea of it made me nervous all over again.

But it was almost too easy to knock on Paul's door (with a pebble, of course) and formally accept his insanely generous offer. Too easy to step into this strange, alien situation; and all the time, behind every word we spoke was the knowledge of my likely infection. It made my skin prickle, like I had a temperature. Even as I reassured Paul that I had everything I needed – God, he was so kind it made my stomach hurt – I made a mental note to talk to Sarah about it tomorrow, this psychosomatic effect. It was one thing reading about it in a psychology text book, but kind of creepy when it happened. Unless I really was coming down with virus symptoms straight away.

I swallowed. *Don't even think about it.*

Once I'd thanked Paul and caught the keys from his underarm throw, it was as if all the distractions of talking to people became a sort of retrospective tension which slipped away as soon as I moved off. That was the business of daytime; this was night. They were two completely separate worlds. Here I was, my trainers clattering the gravel of this garden path which I knew so well, but from another lifetime. The place was the same, but it felt so different, though it was really me that had changed.

And now here I was, sunk into a whole other layer of night. Infected, isolated, in a place I didn't belong, with no idea whether my job would still be there at the end of it all. My throat strained as if all this hideous truth had swelled into a boil in there; as if I'd swallowed my fist.

No, there's much, much worse than this. I cursed under my breath as I locked the church hall door behind me, then remembered that these were church grounds, and cursed some more, silently this time.

Feeling cold and hollow inside, I sat on one of the chairs, flipped open my laptop and went to a news channel.

The virus was spreading fast, taking lives. Crazy numbers were no longer only in China, but in Italy and Spain. The death toll was creeping up in Britain, too. How had it come to this? From a single British carrier who had travelled back from a conference in Singapore, to hundreds of cases. A mere few weeks ago we'd all been focussed on this one case in Brighton, waiting to see how that panned out; now, presumably, several if not dozens more had unknowingly brought the virus into the country, and the infection rate was multiplying fast.

How stupid we were, for carrying on as normal when most carriers had no symptoms for the first several days.

The screen blurred as I let the tears come. I was useless to the world. There was nothing I could besides this: sit here on a church hall chair and stare at a screen while the politicians debated, and the health staff slaved, and people got sick and died.

I cried for them, I cried for my sad, pitiful self for crying for my losses when others had lost so much more. My eyes and my chest burned.

Eventually I had to do something sensible. I had to eat, or I'd wake up hungry in the night.

I laid out my sofa cushions in a row on the floor and tucked the sheet around them – Sarah really had thought of everything – then sat down again to eat the pizza cold. I couldn't be bothered to faff around with the oven. No, that was only part true. The real reason was that none of this was mine to use. I was borrowing someone else's space, and it didn't feel right.

"I'll have to make it feel right soon," I told myself out loud. My words echoed in the near-empty space, and I shivered. Yes, it was a bit cold, but not bad. The room was as wide as our lounge but longer, ending in the kitchen units at the other end, white squares that glared brightly under the light.

I'd have to ask Sarah to bring over my desk lamp tomorrow. The overhead fluorescents were a bit all-or-nothing, and when I finally switched them off, it would be total darkness, except that the light in the garden would probably stream through the window.

I twisted round to look at it. Was it weird that there were no curtains? I'd locked the gate on my way back in. The only person who could let themselves in, besides Paul, was Dale. An image of his face jumped into my mind, the way it had emerged from the shadows. But Dale was a well-meaning bloke, he was fine. A bit odd...*I* was a bit odd.

I was grateful for this place, I told myself, wiping my eyes. This place was a life saver.

Out of nowhere, I found myself thinking: *Would I survive?*

I wasn't ready to think about that yet. My mind rejected it; it was at once too ludicrous and too scary. Instead, I found myself twisting round again, squinting for a glimpse of that little gargoyle figurine in the tree. Why was I thinking about that again now? Maybe it was just the memories of this place...

Oh. That little boy, Kyle.

I remembered the bruises on his arm. My breath caught as I recalled overhearing Paul's voice, kind but firm, checking up on Kyle's 'situation at home'. I was vaguely aware that many of the kids who came to these groups were from difficult backgrounds, though Paul spared me the details. But with Kyle I'd seen the bruises for myself; once, a thumb shape imprinted on his forearm, purple against the brown.

There was something they'd said on the news, speculating about lockdown. There was a woman from a charity saying that abuse victims would find themselves more trapped than ever. Shouldn't they be allowed outside more often than others? But how would you regulate such a thing?

God, poor Kyle. With an ache, a fresh wave of tears streamed down my face, and I let out a small sob. It echoed horribly in the carpet-less hall. Why was I so emotional?

Snivelling, I hurried to the church toilets to blow my nose, and gathered some handfuls of tissues for later. *Get a hold on yourself.* I needed to calm down, meditate.

I settled myself into a chair with the duvet wrapped around my legs and closed my eyes, focussing on my breathing. A slow, gentle rhythm like a calm sea breaking on the shore. In. Out. I began to get drowsy but didn't fight it.

Something flapped past my face, and I jerked back, holding my face. But there was nothing there. I must have fallen asleep; I hadn't realised I was so tired. The fluttering sound persisted, but from somewhere behind me, outside the window. It was only my half-asleep state that made me think it was closer.

It was so bright in here; all I could see in the glass were ghost shapes layered behind my reflection. I switched off the light and stared out.

In the pool of light, a black shape hopped away.

That crow again? *Don't be stupid, there were plenty of crows around here.* But there was something else on the ground: a white lump. An uneven shape, sort of scrunched. A handkerchief? I tutted and reached for the door, groping to get the keys out of my pocket and into the lock. It was silly to worry about going out here on my own. It was a private garden! But the skin all over my back and arms tightened in anticipation. Gingerly, I pressed down the handle and stepped outside.

I forced myself closer to the bone-white puddle of light. A breeze blew, and the screwed-up blob shuddered along the ground: just a ball of paper. I half-turned, ready to go back inside, but something made me as nosy as that crow. I ought to put it in the bin, although even as I told myself this, I knew that wasn't the real reason for bending down and picking it up.

Checking that no-one was watching – what, did I think the crow was going to come back and claim it? – I smoothed the page out, taking in the scrawled handwriting, the crossings out. Whatever it was, it was a first draft. At the top, I saw the one line that should have made me stop right there and mind my own business:

Dear Paul,

I scanned down the page, and suddenly I was breathless. What was this? These weird half lines, meanings struggling to make themselves clear…

It's too much. I'm not built for this sort of work. I'm sorry.

When I said I quit, I meant it. If that means no longer gardening here, then I have to make that choice, with reluctance. My nerves are frayed, I can't handle this anymore.

Dale!

I really shouldn't be reading this…

It feels so close now. Dangerously close. The cloud is growing. The mass grows bigger every day. I'm sorry, you will have to find someone else. Another pair of wings.

What the hell was this? 'Cloud' and 'mass'? Were they code for something – Dale's mental health problems perhaps?

This was deeply private. I had to stop reading now. But I couldn't let go of that crinkled piece of paper. What could he possibly mean by 'Another pair of wings'?

I hope we can still be friends, firm friends. If I can just let some time pass before I make contact again. On this plane, of course.

My eyes flew wide open, fixed on those words: *on this plane*. Hadn't Paul mentioned that earlier? But again, this had to be part of a half-joking language they'd built up between them. If Dale had been in deep therapy with Paul for years, they probably had loads of private, shorthand terms for Dale's worst troubles or fears.

I couldn't, I shouldn't keep reading this. It was wrong.

I read on.

You always said the unknown was the most terrifying thing to face. But I would gladly go back to those days before ~~I knew what I~~.

~~I don't know how~~

Seeing what others don't see is so much worse. You have to be stronger than anyone. I'm not that person. I'm just a gardener, whose curiosity got the better of him.

It's worse than before. I have nothing left to give, I'm empty.

More crossings-out. I flipped it over, my heart thudding in my throat. More scribbles. What was this – poetry?

The Fear is near
Here comes the storm
Where nightmares take their form.

Why had Dale put a capital 'F' in front of 'fear'? I shook my head. A lot of people did that by mistake. This was a bunch of doodles, an afterthought when Dale realised this was a draft to be chucked away. Maybe he was a big sci-fi fan or something and was playing around with their mental health references. But those lines caught my imagination, and I found myself picturing a heavy cloud bursting with… What? Some dark force. Fear itself.

A trickle of cold in my stomach. *Oh God, don't start dreaming up weird fantasies now – not when you're about to go to bed. In a place you've never slept before. Completely alone.*

Jeez, I'd have to turn my laptop on again and watch some cartoons or something. Maybe watch a rerun of *Friends* to bring my mind to normality.

Dale! Remind me to ask you, "What the hell?" next time I see you... But just thinking that gave my stomach another sickly twist. I was the creepy one. I'd trespassed on *his* private thoughts, his draft letter. I wondered if he'd got round to writing the final version, whether he'd put it through Paul's door.

I traipsed back in, almost tripping over the threshold. I just couldn't tear my eyes off that letter. So strange, to write poetry on the back... It really did seem to be about the same thing. Clouds, fear.

I couldn't put it in the bin. I folded it up and tucked it deep inside my jeans pocket.

I half lay in the dark, ending up watching clips of old cartoons for as long as I could. I figured if it was already dark, I might drop off more easily.

I kept slipping into a half-doze. I couldn't decide whether I was looking at the bunched duvet over my knees or at something else: a storm cloud. Even the third time this happened,

I couldn't be bothered to sit up. If I resisted sleep, I'd be a mess in the morning. But the in-between state only worsened as I lay there, willing myself to sleep. The cloud idea grew. At the same time, I had the sensation of something crowding in on me. Flutterings, wing tips, hooked claws. Twice more the wing flapping came close, making me jerk from my almost-sleep. Breathless, I tried to wedge myself upright, but I could no longer be sure if I was awake or just dreaming that I was sitting up.

The image drew closer, and I realised what I'd been keeping at bay all this time. The swell, the roll of slate-coloured clouds. A touch of purple in its darkest part, spreading and deepening like a bruise. It raged, a storm of hurt growing thick. From the heaviest part of the swell, the belly of the cloud, a mass of claws and arms reached, grappling their way out into the naked sky. Each one the colour of grief.

I've never hallucinated. I couldn't know how badly the stress had infected my mind and whether this was a new way of having nightmares whilst being half-awake.

The next day I would know it was real.

The Fear was coming.

Part 2

Nest of Shadows

Up I rose. Into the night sky.

Clouds mushroomed on all sides, and I could no longer tell which way was up or down. How did I get here? But this was one of those flying dreams, that was all. Except that this had the flavour of a nightmare. Something was watching me. The certainty of it slithered along the underside of my skin. How was I supposed to get out of this place?

From the swell of clouds above me came a strange chittering.

The prickles in my neck told me this was not natural. No bird would make that noise, nor would it hide inside a cloud like that.

Terror tightened over my skin. My body was trying to shrink itself, make me smaller and less of a target. What claws or teeth or other horrors waited for me inside that cloud? My stomach writhed. I couldn't bear to see what was hidden in there, yet I had to see it. I couldn't tear myself away. The unknown, the unseen, was a magnet.

A crevice in the soft billows. Eyes wide, I floated closer. My heart thudded with this sickness, this need to know.

Where puffs of ashy vapour retracted into a dark line, a tangle of spindly arms and legs poked out, a murky, greenish-grey. If bats were bigger and had thicker arms and legs… Strange noises, murmurs of intelligence, squeaked and chattered in the mass.

A stray elbow slipped out further than the other limbs. I halted mid-air, floating where I was. My tongue felt like a dried-up old slipper – I wasn't sure I could scream if I needed to. What was it? How could such a creature *be*? Its very existence was nauseating. That curved arm, veined with sinews, the skin mottled yet shiny. When was I going to wake up?

A knuckled, pointed head flicked out of the cloud, and those black eyes dug a new horror into me. With a wet grin, it pulled back its lips over canine teeth and stuck out a long, purple-black tongue.

Noxious gas billowed out from its mouth.

The stench was death. Awfulness. The death of everything. The pointlessness of even bothering to breathe.

I swung back, my head screaming with the need to get away. The nest inside the cloud was unsettled by the movement of this one creature and now the others were scrabbling out of the widening gap. There were dozens, hundreds of them, all elbows and knees and hooked, reaching fingers, shrieking with alarm or delight, I couldn't tell. Out they tumbled. They sprang and swooped in all directions, limber on leathery wings. I fell backwards through the air, useless now – whatever flying or floating ability I'd had now evaporated – and one of the creatures *swicked* past me, sniggering. Claws raked through a part of me I didn't know I had. Twisting in pain even as I plunged, I caught sight of my own grey, leathery body. My torn wing was useless to me now. *I was one of them?* Had I been like that all along? Or had I been transformed? It was the gas, the gas that did it!

But it didn't matter, nothing mattered anymore because I was broken, doomed. I couldn't live as one of those *things*. Repulsed by my own existence I dry-heaved on my way down, cringing but hoping for the sudden impact of the ground that would end it all.

A shaft of golden light streamed across my body, and for an eternal beat I was bathed in a feeling I never deserved – not now, nor at any time before this moment. For two whole seconds, everything was okay. It was better than okay, it was glorious. I was blessed just to take this breath and feel this beautiful life inside me, this hope. A gift to me which I cherished. My heart fell open like a flower.

I blinked awake to a mass of duvet and legs. My own legs. Human. I sat up, sucking in relief like it was in the air, my heart bumping unevenly. But just being awake wasn't enough to shake off that nightmare. The poisonous feeling was still there, engulfing my insides in a bitter smoke. I blinked and saw that sickly-coloured face again in my mind's eye, its wicked tongue unrolled to let the gas seep out… Seeing it again, some part of reality that I'd hidden from myself all of yesterday finally slithered into view: yes, reality. Because whatever the cause of this insane vision – call it stress, bad sleep, some chemical imbalance in my brain – I'd lost my grip on denial. All my silly hopes that *everything would be okay* had fallen aside, and I stared unprotected into the horrors of real life, in broad daylight.

First, I was going to die. If not from coronavirus, then from something else at another time. Everybody dies.

I knew this but hadn't really thought about it much until I'd been exposed to coronavirus.

Second, and this had me mentally swooping downwards again, emptied of my will to fight: my life meant nothing. What had I done with my life? What was I doing? What worth did it have? What was the point of it all, anyway?

I groaned and covered my face.

"Too early for an existential crisis," I murmured, but my attempt at droll humour fell flat. Whether I acknowledged it or not, I was in a crisis. I'd simply managed to distract myself up until now, but here it was, an opened book. Like an idiot I thought Dale's draft letter was a great diversion from my stresses, when all it did was inspire my overactive imagination to dream up the perfect metaphor for the actual horrors that lay in wait for me.

This... fear. Why did it feel so much like poison? Nausea flowed cold-hot under my skin. My gut spasmed. Oh God, I needed the loo! I clambered unsteadily to my feet and ran to the toilets, dizzy with the sudden motion. I didn't recall the distance to the church toilets being quite so far, but that was probably because of these shadows that seemed to reach for me along the sides of the corridor. It was my state of mind that was doing it.

But even after this, the simple act of taking care of my body's needs and washing my hands in the sink, I felt none of the usual reassurance you get when a nightmare begins to fade. As I wandered back to the church hall the taste of adrenaline was still in my mouth.

My feet slowed. What had been that gorgeous moment at the end of the dream, that golden sunlight? I stopped and squeezed my eyes shut, desperate to locate that image again. But now that I was awake and preoccupied with my very real stress, it was hard to recapture more than a glimpse of that hopeful moment.

I put the kettle on and forced myself to have a piece of toast with jam on it. At least I had that: food, a day ahead of me. A fortnight in this place, potentially, but I could only think about one day at a time. What would I do with my day? Surely that's all I had to handle right now. That's what Sarah would say, wasn't it? I wasn't going to sit around feeling sorry for myself.

I stopped chewing, struck by an idea. Could Paul give me something to do? If Dale really had quit, then I could do some work in the garden.

I put another slice of toast on. A pinprick of light glowed inside me.

It was still too early to go knocking on Paul's door. I didn't want to make a nuisance of myself.

I busied myself with tidying up, forcing my limbs to move despite the trickle of dread still tangible in my veins. I swore I could actually feel my stomach squirting acid. At least it had the toast and tea to deal with, or else I'd be dry heaving again.

I hesitated as I flipped open my laptop. Dry heaving *again?* But you can't do that for real while you're asleep.

Still. My stomach was sore enough. The muscles ached, complaining as I moved.

Give me reality, I thought as I clicked onto a news channel, instantly regretting it.

Was this reality? All anyone was talking about was coronavirus. Not enough PPE for nurses and other health workers. A full-blown lockdown was inevitable within a week. Businesses were closing, or trying frantically to sort out provisions for home working. Hospital intakes were going up. Deaths were going up.

My so-called crisis was one tiny blip in a bushfire of other crises. There were people in much, much worse situations than me.

I carried one of the plastic chairs outside and sat in the garden. I watched the sun shift in and out behind wind-pushed clouds, dappling the ground with its hesitant gold.

The clouds were all white and fluffy, but still. I didn't like looking at them, somehow.

Dale didn't come. Of course he didn't come. He'd quit. He posted his letter. Weirdo poet.

I couldn't just sit here, stewing in my own stomach acid. I rummaged through my bag of clothes and found an old vest top that was a bit tight on me. Stretching it, I wrapped it over my nose and mouth and just about knotted the ends together in a lump at the back of my head. Not exactly a surgical mask, but really, I had to take precautions like this, even if I was maintaining a social distance.

Using my elbows and feet again, I nudged and jostled my way through the gate. To my relief the street was quiet: no-one there to witness my terrible handiwork. It was hot and stuffy under the thick layers, but that hardly mattered.

It was a short distance past the church and up Paul's front garden path.

I knocked the same way I did yesterday, with side of a smooth stone. Tension tightened my chest and even the skin on my face. What was I going to say? 'I had a bad dream?' Ridiculous. 'I think I might be hallucinating?' Too extreme. Did I really want to suggest that I was psychotic? He wasn't a doctor, and I definitely didn't want to land up in a GP's surgery which would be full of vulnerable people.

But then, yesterday I had asked Paul an impossible question and he had given me an answer that changed everything.

His muffled voice carried to me from a distance, raised and – terse? I'd never heard him angry before.

I hesitated, half-turning. He had other problems. Other people's and his own. I should take care of myself.

Footsteps made me glance behind me. It was just a woman walking along the other side of the street. Dark hair hooked behind her ears, swinging a shopping bag, and – surrounded by colours?

An aura shifted over her body like a sort of membrane, catching and refracting the light. It was like the skin of a bubble only more hazy-edged. A dark, steely blue shimmered around the belly of the thing, dipping low over her legs and feet. It moved as she moved, unaffected by the pavement. But where it gathered over her head, the bruise colour faded and morphed into a shade of honey. Lower down, the blue darkened to a midnight colour and puckered around a hole. At her left thigh, the ordinariness of her stonewashed jeans flashed through.

She looked at me, her eyebrows pinched together. Why I was staring? And what was that ridiculous attempt at a mask wrapped around my face?

I tore my eyes away and stared instead at Paul's garden, the rosebushes nodding in the wind, Paul's front door. I counted down the seconds, tapping my foot in a pantomime demonstration of what I was actually doing: waiting for Paul to answer the door. When I could bear it no longer, I stole just enough of a glance to see that she was gone. I ducked behind the bushes and peered around them to the street. Was I crazy? Did I want to give myself away? The road stretched quite far in both directions, and if I could see her, she could probably see me too. All she had to do was turn around.

Her membrane-thing continued on with her, blues shifting to purples as she shrank into the distance. What *was* that? Was something happening to me, to my brain? Because it couldn't have been real. It couldn't.

Damn, I was losing my mind. Stress and the prospect of my doomed quarantine had pushed me over the edge.

No. I wouldn't let that happen.

I approached the front door again. From somewhere behind it, Paul's voice rose in an anxious tone. There was no second voice, just a pause. He had to be on the phone. What was he getting so antsy about? Dale?

Even though my legs still felt like putty – or maybe *because* I was in this state – I did something I never would have done before. Not back in the days of my sanity, that grand old age that was only twenty-four hours ago but might have been twenty-four years, the way I felt. I checked behind me for any other passers-by then squeezed between the front corner of Paul's house and the last rosebush. There was a gap along the side of his house which turned out to be a dirt track, a long, narrow walkway hemmed in by a tall fence. Behind the fence, the church's pale stones loomed.

Eavesdropping? *Don't think the word.*

With my back against the side wall, I took a few sidesteps, glancing across to the street, fearing that someone might spot me. But the hedge at the front of his garden grew thick behind those rosebushes, hiding me from view.

Just a couple more steps. A metre or so to my left was the edge of a window. It was open a crack and Paul's voice was clear, almost as close as if he were next to me. I froze, holding my breath.

"He left a letter." Dale. He was talking about Dale! So he really had posted it.

There was silence as the other person spoke.

Paul said, "Even with Dale – we're not enough. This is too big for us. This needs…more."

Another pause. Waiting.

"Someone else? I didn't see anything."

The skin on my back tingled. What was he talking about?

More silence. A sigh.

"I don't know. I'll have to go find Bartok. But there's a complication. There's someone, a friend of mine, self-isolating in the church hall. I know, I know… Hm… Well, yes, that did occur to me, but how on earth could that happen? Dale? No. No. There's wasn't enough time. He'd have to teach her…"

What? Teach me what?

With each breath I sucked through the corset of my mask, wild imaginings danced around my head.

Most likely: I was seeing things. I'd finally cracked. I was desperate for meaning, to find some logical sense in my crazy dreams last night and in the aura I'd just envisioned on that woman. When Paul said vague stuff like this it only helped my imagination create even more bizarre connections.

Or.

Something very real and frightening was going on here. Dale had handed in his notice not just as a gardener but as a participant of some bizarre practice. By some horrid accident I'd entered this other zone – this *other plane* as they'd both called it. I was the 'someone else' Paul's friend had seen there. As I stared at the whirls and knots in the wooden fence, it dawned on me that this was true. Impossible, yet true.

I had shuffled down this narrow track, and that was physical reality. But there was another reality I'd slipped into, another type of in-between place entirely, and I was seeing things I shouldn't. I'd trespassed on some horrible secret.

I was no longer completely... *here*.

Experimentally, I closed my eyes for a second, and a flash of that ugly face poking through the cloud made me almost cry out.

It was still so vivid. I pressed a hand over my chest. My heart was jumping like it wanted to break out and run away.

I continued to stare at the fence, trying to calm myself. Reality was just like this fence, these planks of wood. There was a surface reality – the fence – and that's what we all believed in.

A well-constructed, neatly sanded fence. But there was something else at its core, something living that had a whole other intention: the tree it was made from.

I zoned in on Paul's voice again as it drifted away. He was moving through the house, towards the front.

"I'll go speak to her. Yeah."

I pinned myself against the brick wall, letting the cold roughness press into my back. Keys rattled as they were picked up, their jingle smothered as they were stuffed into a pocket. The sound of the door opening to my right.

My stomach dropped like a stone. *I'll go speak to her?* He meant me, didn't he?

I counted his footsteps retreating up the path until I could hear them no more – he had to be on the pavement now. How long did I have? Twenty seconds, maybe less, before he made it to the church hall and discovered I wasn't there. I was meant to be self-isolating! Visiting Paul was justifiable if I had an urgent reason. But to go on a longer walk… I'd just have to follow him really quietly and pretend I'd been for a very short stroll up the road.

A woman's voice carried over the hedge. "Oh, Paul – lovely to see you."

A delay. I pulled my face mask down so I could breathe properly. *Think, think*. Now my way was blocked. My 'little walk' was getting longer by the second.

I hated coming across as careless, ungrateful, especially to someone like Paul. I could hardly claim cabin fever after just one night.

"And how *are* you?"

Oh God. A real talker. I could hear Paul chatting away in return, in no particular hurry, though I couldn't focus on the words.

Could I get past his front door without being seen? I couldn't remember if there was a way through to the next-door garden on the other side.

With every beat that thundered in my chest my fake walk grew more unreasonable. Off I went, strolling across town in happy-go-lucky denial...

From behind me, somewhere in Paul's back garden, a crow barked three times. An answer came, its friend cawing back an echo either from the church roof or the gardens outside the church hall – where I should be.

I straightened up. I had to get over those fences. It was insane, but it was my only face-saving way out.

I jogged down the narrow walkway, the brickwork grazing my elbow. Was I really doing this? I wasn't ten years old anymore! But my feet were still moving, so…

There was the crow, its head tilted to watch me with its beady eye. It cawed again and hopped, flapping awkwardly along the length of the fence. I had no time to wonder how well Dale might have trained these friendly birds because I was searching, searching for a clear way over. Would my jeans snag on the rough ledge? Would I get tell-tale cuts or splinters on my palms? Did I even have the strength to launch myself over this without snapping the wood?

The crow hopped again, barking at me as if demanding my attention. I was unwelcome in his territory – so what? But it made me glance up. Where he now perched was right near the back of Paul's garden. Beneath him and half-hidden by a bush stood a compost bin, wedged against the fence. A stepping stone.

Seeing me look, the crow barked once more and flapped off onto the church roof where he sat and waited.

Oh my God. I'd been hallucinating enough, thank you very much. I didn't need more crazy ideas like birds telling me what to do. Oh well, at least this delusion was actually helpful and didn't involve anything scary.

I jogged over to the bin and pressed my knee onto the lid. The slippery surface meant there was no time to hold myself steady, so I clambered and hauled myself over. I caught myself on the ground on all fours, the impact shuddering up my wrists, but most of my weight on my feet. I shook out my hands and checked behind me: my ungraceful scramble hadn't caused any obvious damage to me or the fence.

One down. *Keep chatting, neighbour.* I did *not* want Paul to stroll into the church hall gardens to catch me launching myself over the fence.

I took a deep breath, eyes fixed on my next hurdle: a fence just as tall as the one I'd cleared. No stepping stone this time. I'd trapped myself, hadn't I? I had no choice but to take a running jump and throw myself over.

No time to think about it.

I bent forward like a runner waiting for the starting pistol. From the slopes of the church roof next to me, the crow cawed. *What now?*

With a jump and a flutter of its black wings the bird rose from its perch and soared across. It landed on the furthest end of the fence which was covered in a creeping plant.

In a head-dipping motion he cawed twice.

Oh, holy… Was that a gate?

"Are you serious?" I whispered. "How can this keep happening? Are you really that brainy?"

Nerves ringing in my limbs, I stumbled over to check it out. It was definitely a gate, though it was so overgrown it couldn't have been used in years. It took some effort to disengage the huge swathe of creeper which hugged the shape of the fence and was heavy besides. Finally, I managed to shove and kick my way through the gate, arms aching and breath sawing as I levered the plant over my head.

Why so breathless? Wildflowers swayed strangely under my feet, and I grabbed the gate to stop myself falling over.

My pulse thumped in my temples. I couldn't get quite enough air.

Was I getting sick? Was this what it was like, at the beginning of the coronavirus?

Footsteps scrunched on the gravel at the far end of the gardens, by the hall. I had to stop fretting and also stop trampling over these goddamn flowers and get onto that path.

I tiptoed as best I could around the plants. How to appear and how to feel normal: this was really all I was thinking about in that moment.

But then I looked up and saw Paul.

At first, I thought I was looking at a patch of sunlight. It was now clear that my hallucinations had gone one step further.

Paul *glowed*. All of him was cloaked in a golden orb, except that it was oval, dropping right over his body. Just like that woman in the street. His aura moved with him as he strolled towards me.

All I could do was stand and gawp.

"Elina?" he called, and his voice pierced my dumbstruck fixation.

You're staring again. Pretend that everything's normal.

"Paul. I… was going to come and see you, but figured you'd be busy."

"Hi," he said as if he hadn't quite processed what I'd said. He was looking at me, head on one side. Assessing me. His kind, dark eyes swept over my body as if he could see some troubled sign in my posture.

Unless he could see what I was seeing, on me.

I had a flashback to yesterday evening, of Dale's face emerging from the back of the garden, not far from where I stood. His eyes had grazed the area around me rather than looking at me directly. Was he seeing what I now saw?

No. Don't give in to these crazy ideas. Then normality really will be a distant dream.

But – Paul was golden. The membrane that enveloped him was breath-taking. Like seeing the sunlight quiver on the ground when all you've had is darkness and rain for months. Like – those rays of golden light I saw when I was on the other plane? What did it all mean?

It was hard to look away until I reminded myself that he might get the wrong message if I pored over him for a second longer.

I focussed on the garden, smiling as best I could as if to say, 'Isn't this place lovely?' while I picked my way along the path towards him.

But Paul wasn't going to be fooled. "Is everything okay?"

I sighed, pulling my mask over my mouth again and plonking myself down on the tree stump. Let him take the bench this time.

"Bad dreams. *Really* bad dreams. I mean, extremely vivid and frightening. There were these *creatures…*" I shuddered, feeling that nausea swirl up inside me again, its bitter bile.

It took a moment for Paul to clock that I'd given him the bench. He lowered himself into it slowly, his brow crossed with concern.

No. I *wasn't* going to draw some weird connection between the conversation I'd just overheard and the hellish images I'd had last night; nor with this weird, visual cortex problem I clearly had, that made his golden light seem to pulse as I looked at him. *Don't look.*

"Bad dreams," he echoed. He nodded as if reassured by this idea although he kept snatching odd looks at me: at my knee, my waist, my ear.

"I guess it's the stress, and the weirdness of everything," I said, warming to this tale. It did make me feel better, to consider that this was the real way to understand it all. I still had a grip on reality, yes. Despite what my eyes kept telling me, and the strange behaviour of certain local crows – I threw a suspicious glance at the fence and the crest of the church roof next door, though the birds were nowhere to be seen – I was still a part of the real world. My eyes and my brain could play tricks on me all they liked, although I really hoped they would stop doing that very, very soon.

Paul's brow furrowed deeper as he nodded. "It's difficult, very difficult. There's so much fear about. These are new, unfamiliar stresses we have to deal with, with this pandemic. People are not used to thinking about their mortality like this."

"Do you think that's what it was?" I asked. How quickly we had landed on the core of it: death.

"Could be," he said. "But what exactly did you see last night, Elina?" It sounded like a statement, his tone was so flat and resigned. But there was just an undercurrent of danger behind those words. The possibility rose inside me again with the flutter of a panicked bird. I remembered what he'd said over the phone: 'Someone else? I didn't see anything.' Then mentioning me as a 'complication'. But the very idea that he was checking whether I'd trespassed on this *other plane* of his was utterly bonkers.

In that case, there's no harm in telling the truth. My stomach plunged at the idea, but it was true. Surely Paul had seen his fair share of people with mental health problems. There was likely nothing he hadn't come across before.

"I… had this vision of being drawn up into the sky. I saw these creatures, they were disgusting. Sort of like goblins, all huddled up inside a cloud. Then they breathed out this hideous smoke that made me feel awful. Then one of them attacked me and I realised… I was one of them."

Paul seemed to be holding his breath throughout, but at this last part his mouth popped open.

"One of them? How could you – ?" He stopped, gathered himself. "What *part* of yourself did you see?"

Well, that was a weird question to ask. "My wing. One of them tore through my... wing." I turned and looked to my right shoulder. The place where I'd seen it.

Paul was rigid for a few seconds, his expression unreadable. Suddenly he broke into a smile. "It's okay. It's just a dream."

"It is?" I blurted, wishing I hadn't. How could I act surprised at that?

Paul was serious again, but his frown was easier, less suspicious. He was showing the proportionate amount of concern for an ailing friend. "Sorry, I didn't mean to say 'just'. Dreams can be powerful things. Sometimes they're our messengers from the unconscious mind."

He leant forward, his forearms on his lap. There was more coming. *Relax, don't look too freaked out and he'll spill.*

"It's this situation with the coronavirus. It's so new to us. Fear of mortality has intensified and pretty much everyone is feeling the same things right now." He opened his hands. "As a culture, we are not very well prepared for this. We don't often discuss or even think about our own deaths. Have you heard of the collective unconscious?"

Was this it? Was he telling me? But this sounded like a psychological theory.

"Erm, vaguely. I don't think it came up in my A-level course, but I've definitely heard of it."

Paul gave a quick smile. It had to be odd, him having to explain a major theory to 'The Psychologist' as he often called me, but neither of us was in the mood for our usual banter.

"Carl Jung was a bit of a maverick so it doesn't hold water with a lot of psychologists even nowadays, but the theory is an interesting one: that a deeper, universal part of our minds exists. The source of universal ideas, linking us all together. Archetypes like the trickster, the hero and even the Great Flood crop up again and again throughout history, across all cultures – and way before the internet, when there was no way of those ideas travelling." He smiled. "Sometimes, usually under stress, we get a glimpse, or an eyeful. And so the unconscious becomes conscious."

Wait. That was it? A psychological theory?

"My dream seemed so real," I said, pressing him to say more.

"Dreams give us a window to our personal unconscious but sometimes the universal, collective one too."

It wasn't enough. I knew now, with a slick sensation in my very skin, that Paul was holding back. He had a secret. It was too big and powerful for the likes of me. I'd stumbled into it uninvited, and now he was trying to fob me off with a textbook hypothesis.

I burned with curiosity. Perhaps I'd had just enough of a break from sickened terror and jumping over fences for my brain to pull back and think, 'Huh?'

While I was dicing with what to say next – how much to say – those words I'd heard him almost shout over the phone echoed back to me: 'Even with Dale – we're not enough. This is too big for us…'

There was definitely something going on here. Something dangerous. Enormous. The idea that I might be part of something that went beyond the confines of my pathetic, meaningless little life made me ache to know more.

Could I really admit I'd been snooping on him, on top of everything else?

There was one confession that might tip things over the edge, make him realise he had to tell me everything.

"But, Paul. Since the dream, you look... different to me."

He sat up straighter. "Different how?"

I forced myself to look at his hair, which was cut short as usual. His sweater, which was green and nothing out of the ordinary. But we both knew I was stalling, measuring his reaction. I wasn't referring to his clothes, his appearance. I meant – that *other* thing.

"There's a golden haze all around you."

Paul took in a breath. Now I'd started, I wasn't going to stop.

"I saw someone else as well. Passing in the street. She had a sort of bluish membrane around them like a giant bubble. And there was a hole in it – "

"Stop." Paul stood up. His hands tightened and shook at his sides. Was he angry?

"Paul, you have to tell me what's going on."

"How did he let you in?"

"How did who – ?" But even as I began, I knew. He meant Dale.

I reached into my jeans pocket. I'd folded the letter several times, and now it resembled a tight rectangle, warm from being in my pocket for so long. With clumsy hands I unfolded it and held out the crumpled piece of paper for his inspection.

Paul didn't touch it, though he leaned in slightly closer than he ought to, his shocked eyes darting back and forth over the scrawled handwriting.

"I need to make a phone call. Please excuse me for a few minutes."

He might have only been gone for half an hour. But time was different to me now. Every second pulsed with this new reality.

That look Paul had given me and the piece of paper in my hand. That's what told me this was real.

There was another plane. I'd been on it. I'd... flown through it, seen things I shouldn't have seen.

What could I do, besides wait here and hope that he'd answer all my questions when he came back? I wasn't going to go scrambling over fences again so I could listen in on his clandestine phone calls, though I thirsted to know more. More about these other people he spoke to, who knew about that other place. More about Dale and why he'd bowed out of this thing so suddenly.

The letter shook in my hand, but I folded it up and tucked it away again. I didn't need to re-read it to remember how disturbed Dale was: the desperate tone of his writing, the weird hints and poetry he'd scribbled on the back. Things that had somehow led to me going to that place. But how?

Paul had at least left me with instructions: to spend these minutes alone focussing my mind on something in nature. He pointed at the flowers, the oak tree, a leaf scattered onto the ground.

"Anchor your mind here, in the simplicities of this reality." What was I supposed to make of that?

As he'd turned and hurried up the path, I saw the blue patch emerging in his golden membrane. A hole opening. I knew without asking that this was Fear. My uninvited blunder into that other place had made Paul feel afraid.

I tried to meditate like he told me, but my heart kept bouncing about. Trying to focus my mind here and now only brought the hellishness of my situation home: a part of me was still *there*. I only had to blink for more than a second and that pointed, leathery face was glaring at me again. Clouds roved around me in great gusts. I held my breath, frightened to take in any more of that poisonous gas.

I jigged on my seat, then stood up and paced about. I felt like the waiting was going to split my brain in half. How long was Paul going to be? Who was he calling, and what were they going to *do* with me now I knew their secret world?

Hands still shaking, I pulled out my phone and pressed Sarah's number.

The ring tone beat at me. One, two. One, two. Could I tell her? How? No, I needed normality. Just a little slice of comfort before I plunged backwards into the unknown.

"Sarah? Oh, are you having your lunch? Sorry…"

I asked her about her lab tests. We talked about the news, the weirdness of everything. I teased her about working on a Saturday. We even talked about the weather. Anything but this.

"So, they're letting me off early," she said. "The queues for supermarkets are just insane, and my boss knows I'm shopping for you too. I hope I can get enough toilet roll; people are just going crazy for it right now…"

'Insane.' 'Crazy.' She had no idea.

When I heard the gate clang, I wrapped up the call quickly. Sarah would be over later. I only had a small window of time to demand an explanation from Paul, and to build up a better semblance of 'normal' by the time Sarah arrived with the shopping.

I stood up as Paul strode towards me. "What's going on? What does all of this mean?"

He stopped the recommended two metres away and spread his hands in a 'calm down' gesture. "It's okay, Elina. I've spoken to the others I work with. They all agree, this is not your burden to carry, okay? This is not your burden to carry."

What did that mean, and why did he say it twice?

Paul's eyes hardened at the phone in my hand. "You haven't told anyone else, have you?"

"No. As if they'd believe me!" I spluttered. But I was clinging to his previous words. Could it really be true? That this thing – whatever it was – wasn't 'my burden'? It felt like I was being let off the hook, although I still needed to know what that meant.

Paul seemed to read my thoughts, though his expression was warm and relaxed. "I'll explain it to you – but only as much as you need to know. Think of it as a strange fairy tale, because that's all it has to be, to you. Please understand. I'm trying to protect you. And protect you I shall.

"There are realities which exist beyond the one that surrounds us now. What you are experiencing now, these visions, these colours," he swept a hand in front of his torso where the golden membrane still glowed, "will fade in time. You just need to meditate on the natural things of this world, to draw yourself back here, fully and completely. I will help you do this. Everything is going to be okay. Trust me."

"But... how can you be sure?" There were a million questions I wanted to ask, but more than anything I craved his reassurance.

Paul sat down on one end of the bench and indicated for me to sit at the other. "You have seen inside a part of your mind that you don't normally see. That includes a glimpse of a gateway into the collective unconscious. That's why it's like a fairy tale. And we can treat it like that, okay? Together, we'll make it so."

"A *bad* fairy tale," I said.

"A *very* bad fairy tale." He actually chuckled.

There was a light thump on the top of the fence. A crow cawed at us, bobbing its head in time.

Paul smiled. "Bartok! Good to see you."

"Bartok?" I frowned. Where had I heard that name before?

Paul held out his wrist, and the bird swooped over to land on it. It was strange to see the creature close up, and obviously tame. The sunlight stroked its feathers a beautiful purple-black.

"Dale and I named them after classical composers. Dale's is called Sibelius." His smile dropped and he pursed his lips against other, unsaid words while he ran the back of his finger along Bartok's wing.

His wing. Was it just a coincidence, this connection with winged creatures? Dale had written something like, 'We need another pair of wings.'

"So, Paul," I began, trying to tame the quaver in my voice and sound as casual as I could. "This… fairy tale of yours. Does it involve crows?"

Paul watched my face carefully, checking for signs of fear or… serious belief? How much was he prepared to tell me? More, if I played along with this game.

He'd already promised to explain it to me. Enough to make it all make sense. Enough to quash my curiosity and anchor me firmly in this world.

I kept my smile easy, and busied myself admiring Bartok's handsome feathers.

"Well," said Paul, "as the story goes… You can't enter that other realm physically unless you are ghosted."

"Ghosted?"

"No, *hosted.*"

I blinked quickly. Everything was taking on a second meaning. Everything was *ghosted* with a second layer, a sickening idea shifting out from under the real thing, like a shadow that had a life of its own; a separate, sly intention that had nothing to do with ordinary life. The antithesis of normality.

But I had to at least pretend to be part of the world of normality, just to get this 'story' out of Paul. Did he really think he could fob me off with this fairy tale idea?

I was depending on it.

"That's…" There were no words. Maybe this really was beyond anything I could believe. "So he's like your avatar or something? In the story," I added quickly.

"Something like that. Crows, like all animals, occupy the material and mental-spiritual planes at the same time. They don't differentiate. In fact, they consider us rather strange for having separated ourselves from the unconscious realms – a result of our so-called 'intelligence', you know? We've come to control so much of our conscious world, built artificial environments like houses instead of surrendering to nature and surviving against the elements. In the process we've lost our awareness of the natural energies and planes that exist beyond it."

I didn't know what to say. I stared at Bartok, his proud and slightly mocking gestures as he bobbed up and down. "It's like he understands you."

"When my psyche piggybacks his, we have an understanding," Paul said quietly, his voice brimming with secrets. There was a privacy, an intimacy in this strange connection he had with Bartok. The hairs on my arms sprung up. It was too strange but also – sort of awesome.

"And," Paul said, coming out of his reverie to address me, "none of the crow hosts have broken their right wing. So there's no way you rode any of them. It's all in your imagination." He beamed. "And that's where all of this can stay."

We wandered up the path together – well, I was two paces ahead – taking in the simple beauty of the garden, the way the plants all reached up for the golden light. Is that what my mind was trying to do? Was that what the golden lights of my vision meant? Why, then, had it managed to find so much darkness?

Was Paul really expecting me to accept and move on from all of this? Even if I could, he'd made it clear that the collective unconscious was a tangible thing, a place; or, the 'gateway' to it certainly was. My skin began to creep again with a new ferocity. All these questions gathered at my throat, a ball too tight to swallow.

I turned to watch Paul taking one slow step after another, frowning at his shoes as if he were concentrating really hard on something. What if he was in some sort of denial? What if he just couldn't face the idea of me becoming a part of this otherworldly horror – perhaps a new and rather big responsibility for him to deal with at a time of worsening stress – and so he clung to this one fact, the lack of a crow host, as being proof that I'd got out scot-free?

In that case, how come I could see his aura?

The garden was so peaceful around us now that the wind had died down. An empty sort of peacefulness. As the sun opened its eye on the scene, each flower, each blade of grass hid a shadow on its other side.

"Paul..." I had to tell him, I had to explain my train of thoughts, in case we were both beginning to operate under a false sense of security.

He looked up, waiting. I glanced across at the tree where the little clay gargoyle sat: Kyle's gargoyle. The boy with the bruises whom I'd helped so little, so long ago. A pang of grief shot through me, and an odd feeling of connection. Suddenly I wanted to rush over to the clay model and comfort it, as if this would somehow reach Kyle himself and make him feel better. With a nationwide lockdown almost upon us, Kyle was about to be trapped in his very own nightmare – unless something had actually come of those social services visits and he and his mum had been able to move away from his abusive father.

"What is it?" said Paul. He watched me staring at the gargoyle.

The clay model. It was...

Virus be damned – I picked up the gargoyle and swivelled it around so Paul could see what I saw.

"The wing. Look. The wing is broken!"

Part 3

Conversations with Crows

We stood staring at the gargoyle in my hands. It was a piece of clay. A dead object. I hadn't even crafted it myself. Yet I'd been inside it – I'd *been* it, flapping through the air, tumbling to the ground. I remembered breaking my wing. Its wing.

I thought I'd been turned into one of those hideous, cloud-nesting creatures... but I'd been *this*.

"How?" said Paul. There seemed nothing else to say.

"Dale?" I reminded him.

Paul shook his head, unable to tear his eyes off the gargoyle. "It's not enough. It's not enough to do *this*. Impossible... This piece of clay doesn't have a *mind*."

The sun came out. Around us, the garden glowed with renewed colour: the nodding heads of flowers, the neatly clipped grass. Even the gravestones at the back looked cheerful as if they were part of some children's story, a fable where goodness would challenge evil and then win.

But Paul and I stood in an invisible shadow of our forbidden knowledge, cold and rigid while the outside world moved with its gentle warmth. Normal reality was far beyond us now. Fear in its purest, primal form was just a blink away, and I knew it to be real.

Paul blinked as if struggling against the spell of stillness. "I don't know how Dale did this. Without the proper rituals you'd never be able to enter a crow's mind."

"The crow? This is ridiculous…"

Paul raised his eyebrows. "More ridiculous than you being hosted by a clay model?"

"Okay then – *how?*"

He sniffed and shook his head. "What Dale wrote was a kind of invitation. Those hints. That *poetry*. He deliberately left out details, knowing that your imagination would step in and finish the story. That was enough to draw your mind upwards, to find out for yourself."

"You mean this was deliberate? Dale planted that letter there, hoping that I'd pick it up and read it?" The idea thudded in my chest, a sickly beat. That also meant that he'd got the crow to flap around and make a noise, to try and get my attention. He *had* been watching that evening as I'd crept outside in the dark. I shuddered, rubbing my arms.

At length Paul said quietly, "Dale has broken the most fundamental rules of our pact. He has Intrigued you." He said it like it had a capital 'I'. "He found a gap in your consciousness, your Fear. It's possible he tried to prime Sibelius to host you, but… he can't have been expecting *this*, surely…."

I stared at Paul's crow, Bartok, who waddled along the grass pecking at insects. He glanced up intermittently as if half-interested in our talk. But that was crazy. As if he could understand!

Suddenly Paul was frowning, pointing at the gargoyle. "Who made this? Did you make this?"

"No. A boy called Kyle."

"Kyle. Sounds familiar."

"He was in our group. The arts and crafts group. The boy with the…bruises."

Paul froze. Something passed through his eyes. It was like seeing his thoughts, or the colour of his thoughts. Maybe it was the effect of seeing his aura which flexed from gold to blue as he stared at – something, far beyond me.

"I wonder," he said, his jaw tight. "I should check he's okay, just in case. It doesn't really make any sense, but…" He stared at the model in my trembling hand. "He may have been affected by this."

"What? How?" The idea that I might have hurt Kyle – no, it couldn't be. But a wave of coldness rose up through my skin, telling me it was possible.

"By using something he made with his own hands…" Paul squeezed his forehead, uncertain. "Kyle put thought and emotion into this, as a piece of art. But no, this has more to do with *your* mind. What does this model represent to you, Elina?"

"Well, it's Kyle's, isn't it? And I'm worried about him. Scared. That thing they said on the news about abuse victims in lockdown. And lockdown is happening, isn't it?"

Paul was quiet, brooding. "I believe so. By the end of this week, or perhaps the beginning of next week, yes. It's inevitable now."

"You don't really think I've hurt Kyle, do you?"

Paul pinched his eyes and exhaled slowly through his nose. "I… don't think so. But there's no harm in giving his mother a quick call just to say hi. She'll be on my list of contacts…"

"What do I do?"

Paul's sorry eyes grazed over me. "You are one of us now."

I swallowed. "You make it sound like there's no going back."

Paul nodded. "It's too late. You have seen and you have... been seen. The beasts of the other plane know you now. They've watched you watching them. They will haunt you now. You are one of us. Whether we like it or not."

"We?" It sounded like a weak reply, but it was loaded with the need to know. He didn't mean just us two, did he? There were others involved. The person he'd rung earlier today. Others, most likely. This thing was big. Too big, even for them, from what I'd overheard.

If I was part of it now, with no chance of going back, he had no choice, did he? He had to tell me everything.

Paul was business-like all of a sudden. "There's much you need to learn. I think in the circumstances, we need to act quickly. I'll see if I can get hold of Mel, our leader, on a video conference. You have a laptop with you." He looked at me sharply, needing to confirm this.

"Yes. Yes, I'll go charge it up."

In the distance, the gate squeaked then clanged.

Paul and I stared at each other. "Sarah," I said, moving only my lips.

"I've got phone calls to make," Paul whispered, moving off. "Don't let her stay for too long, we need to get going with this."

Without turning, I stood and listened to his footsteps retreating and Sarah's quiet approach. Their cheery 'hi' and 'hello' floated to me from a long way off, or so it felt; a conversation of polite, mutual introduction that seemed a great distance away, broken sentences carried to me on the wind.

I was a thousand miles from normal. I had to get back to who I was, in this reality, and fast. Or at least pretend. Sarah couldn't know that something was *this* wrong. She'd panic, ask too many questions, and I'd end up telling her the truth – which was utterly barmy and dangerous besides.

I was still holding the gargoyle. I lay it gently between the two limbs of the tree, resting it against its broken wing so it wouldn't fall off completely. This was where it belonged, for now. I made a mental note to order some decent crafting glue online and fix it, but that would have to be later. Much later. Right now, I needed to create a distance between myself and this object. It held some kind of power over me, that much was clear.

The need to turn around nagged at me. Sarah's hair and her shopping bags were light colours hovering in the gaps between the branches of the big tree. But wait – how 'normal' could I be expected to be in the circumstances? And how much did it really matter, as long as I didn't go 'do a Dale' and tell Sarah the weird details? And, by the way, at what point was I going to have the chance to ask Dale what the hell he was thinking?

Sarah waited to one side of the path while Paul passed, shaking her head at his offer to help with the shopping – I supposed that was wise, although she was wearing a mask anyway – then she bustled along the short distance to the door of the church hall. Even from here I could see the weight of the two swollen bags by the way she dumped them on the ground. It looked like she'd bought me enough to last a week.

I hurried down the path. "Sarah, you're so kind. You didn't have to get so much!"

Her voice was a bit muffled by her mask. "Don't worry. How's it going? What is that *thing* you're wearing on your face? I got you some masks," she said, pointing a thumb back at the swollen bags. "Proper ones. And some alcohol gel."

"Thanks," I said, a little taken aback by the strange new aura that swirled around her. This was going to take some getting used to. The blues twisted around greens and greys, like her uncertainty was arguing with itself. It felt like an intrusion of her privacy, to see her anxieties for me rove around so plainly for me to see.

She stood watching me. The dark blues deepened as she took in my face – what she could see of it, anyway. "So, how's it going…?"

Who was I kidding? I was a mess.

"I… I guess I've been struggling a bit." I coughed, trying to swallow back the ball of tension in my throat. "I've been having nightmares." As I said this, something clicked into place. Why shouldn't I tell her a few hints of what I was going through? Nothing visual like Dale, no – nothing like that. But the way Paul played the 'story' card with me and told me stuff without really saying anything as fact. Could I do I little bit of that with Sarah? Her imagination wasn't ridiculous like mine, and I wasn't going to imply any of it was materially real.

"Nightmares?" she echoed, her forehead scrunched with worry. Her voice sounded so small. "Like what?"

"Like I was seeing Fear itself. Staring into the eyes of Fear itself. Creatures…" I rubbed my head and stared at the ground, idly wondering how far I could take this while my mouth just kept going. "I guess I don't realise half the time what I must be feeling underneath."

I finally dared look up. But Sarah was nodding.

"Everything's changed. Everything's weird and wrong. Loads of people are feeling what you feel, I'm sure of it."

It wasn't enough. She was my friend, my counsellor. Why shouldn't I tell her more?

"To be honest, I feel like I'm on another plane of existence. That nothing's real any more. Or like a whole load of things which shouldn't be real, are. Like actual monsters." My voice cracked. I felt lightheaded with the possibility of actually telling her. Without Paul around to warn me and hold me back, how much was I going to let slip? The temptation to tell Sarah was like falling upwards. The same sensation I got when I closed my eyes. "The monsters – in my mind – are like these strange, long-fingered, horn-headed *goblins*…" I swallowed. "I know that sounds ridiculous, but I'm scared. They're real, on some level."

"Elina." Sarah studied me. Her eyes were patient; she didn't buy it. Well, of course she didn't buy it. I didn't really want her to, did I?

Maybe partly. Maybe just a little.

"Elina, we both know there's a part of you that's revelling in this."

"What?" Did I just hear her right?

"Elina, you know this already. This is you. How many times have we discussed this – how many packets of biscuits have we demolished…?"

"…whilst saying *what?*"

She sucked in a breath. It caused her mask to pull in at the front. I wondered, not for the first time, how close she'd got to rolling her eyes at me and how much effort it took to stop herself. Definitely not for the first time. "I think a part of you wants the bizarre. You don't want things to be normal, because that would just be – normal." She lifted and dropped her arms in a half-hearted shrug. "You can't hack the normal. Why should you?"

My eyes stung, though the familiarity of what she said beat back at me. I wasn't going to blink, because that would be admitting it; that would make the tears roll down my cheeks and there'd be no denying it.

"And why not?" I tilted my head at her in mock inquiry, or maybe it really was a genuine question. I both hated and loved the fact that she could say these things to me. To know me so completely. Yet I needed to hear it once more. How easily I'd forgotten, been swept up in all this stress and strangeness.

"Because accepting normal would be like accepting that it's all okay. It would like saying, 'Yeah, okay, I do like this job. I like the fact that I never made it as an artist.' Your dreams were bulldozed over, Elina, by normality. And it'll be a long time – if ever – before you forgive it."

I allowed myself a blink, training my eyes on the ground while two wet lines trickled down my cheeks.

"I'm sorry, Elina." Now her voice was warm, thick with emotion. "I wish I could hug you right now. I guess it's all getting a bit much at the moment. I do miss you. But you know I'll always tell you the truth," she added, a hint of humour creeping in. "And I still believe that one day you'll find a healthy outlet for your weirdness. One that doesn't freak you out even more. It's crises like these that tell me you *will make it* as an artist one day."

"But why? How?" It sounded petulant; my voice high pitched like a whining child.

"Because you still need it. You haven't actually given up. Sometimes you think you have, but you haven't. That's what all this crazy stuff means." She shrugged, properly now, with both shoulders. "If you could accept your normal job and be absolutely, truly fine with it – *then* I would be seriously worried."

After Sarah left, I remembered the laptop. I plugged in the charger without bothering to check how much juice it had left already.

The sound of Paul's heavy stride on the gravel path had me hurrying outside again. Seeing him again, my thoughts jumped straight back to Kyle.

"Well? Is he okay?"

Paul was gently shaking his head. *Oh no. No, no.* But his expression was mild. "No-one answered. I didn't leave a message… Elina, you need to calm down. You've done nothing wrong."

I backed away up the path, afraid that he was going to reach out and touch my shoulder, come too close. He sighed, arms drooping, and I remembered the shopping.

"Take one of the masks from my bag. Please. I haven't been near any of it yet. Please, Paul."

Seeing no reason to refuse, Paul meandered over to the bags and poked around until he found a mask. From the colour it looked to be medical-style, just like Sarah's.

On his way back to the bench he dropped a second mask onto my tree stump, beckoning me over.

"Oh. Thanks." As I sat down and switched my hideous face wrapping for an actual, comfortable mask, my head was busy with what Sarah had said. My refusal to accept normality. My weirdness. Well, maybe there was something in that.

"It's something in me, isn't it? It's something in me that's caused this to happen. It's not…" I wanted to say, 'It's not like I thought I was 'special' or powerful or anything.' Surely it was the very opposite. "It's a sort of weakness, isn't it?"

Paul was curious. "Why would you say that?"

"It has to be. I didn't do what you do, not properly. If Dale really tried to get me to enter that place, and even prepped his crow for it… Well, that didn't work, did it? I did something weird instead. I screwed up."

Paul took his time to answer, pinching his mask to fit over the bridge of his nose. "The only thing I can think of – the only thing that could've made a piece of clay come alive, not that I've ever heard of such a thing, is empathy. Your empathy for Kyle." He regarded me seriously. "Feeling is not a weakness, Elina. It's what makes us human. And compassion – compassion is the better part of us. Never regret that part! It's a powerful thing, and it's actually at the heart of what *we* do. But I see what you mean and, yes, your fear has made you vulnerable to this. Perhaps the intensity of what's going on right now has opened you up." He wagged his head at this impossible thing. "You ended up on the other plane, riding your empathy; a symbol of your fear." He sat upright, looking around. "Is your laptop charged?"

"Oh. Sorry." I hurried to the hall and brought the laptop back, cradling it under my arm.

I sat half on the path, half on the grass so I could steer the screen towards us both. Paul directed me to an online chat service for which I already had a login. While we waited for it all to load, he filled me in on what I'd been itching to hear, although it sounded like a strange, ancient mythology enriched by his storyteller's voice.

"There is nothing in this world besides love and fear. When you enter the other plane, this is what you see manifested. It is the layer between layers: the layer between the material reality, what is processed and understood by our minds as personal individuals; and the place beyond that, the collective unconscious, the level on which all timeless and universal understanding derives.

"And so what remains an abstract concept to most people – fear, love, faith, hope – becomes a physical reality to us.

"What we Watchers do is twofold…"

I thrilled at this title but was careful to keep my expression straight. It made them – us! – sound like comic book heroes.

Paul continued. "We maintain the protective membrane that keeps the very worst of our fear at bay – that is, Fear with a capital 'F'. Those of us with crow-hosts fly closer to the membrane to inspect the holes that open and grow, and either mend them or guard them as best we can."

"Membrane? What's that? All I saw were clouds, and those creatures."

"A bit of practice and concentration and you'll be able to see it. As above, so below," Paul said, opening his hands over the personal membrane that still glowed around him. He seemed calmer; maybe that was why the bluish parts had retracted and been replaced by gold.

"Our minds and spirits – our psyches – are each protected individually, cushioned from life's hard knocks, you might say, by love and hope. It's just that general sense of wellbeing we have in the background. It's generated by a mixture of different things for different people, but mostly it comes from the feeling of being loved or worthy of love; and this naturally reflects back at others, in our compassion. You might compare it to the way a colour both absorbs and reflects back light."

"Oh," I said. "The gold does kind of shimmer…"

"Yes." I imagined that under that mask Paul's mouth quirked up at the corner at this, but I had to make do with his eyes which were still serious but softened. "The universal membrane works in the same way except that it's… universal. What we feel, how protected we feel overall, affects how strong it is and how big the holes get – and how much Fear gets through. Of course, there are other primal forces which come through, because the other plane is the gateway to the collective unconscious."

"Oh. Such as…?"

"Archetypal ideas. Symbolic truths that have been inherent in/out thinking since the beginning of human memory, like God, the Mother, the Shadow, the Trickster. Even artistic inspiration."

"Wow." I could hardly imagine what that would look like. "Do you get to *see* that too?"

Paul bobbed his head, not meeting my eyes. "We can, and we do, but it is not good to focus on these other… shapes of thought. When Mel takes you through the process, you must learn to respect your limits; our limits. If we let ourselves get caught up in all that is visible on that plane, it's easy to get lost and lose sight of what we are trying to do: keep Fear at bay. Protect people from the worst of it."

"Can't you get rid of Fear completely? I mean, if you got enough people on to it…"

"Fear can never be obliterated. It is the other side of love; the two potent forces at the bottom of all things. This is why they are so vivid on the other plane, compared to the other thought-shapes. All flows from love and Fear. Ah, if you can just type in Mel's account…"

"What? Oh." I'd almost forgotten about the online chat, this ordinary thing we were trying to do. It was weird that we had to communicate through laptops or phones when the Watchers spent their time doing mind-travel. Then again, maybe it was limited to crows – or clay models, apparently.

Paul spelled out the account name, and we sat and waited, listening to the electronic ringing sound.

"Why can't I see my own membrane?" I wasn't sure if there was time for him to answer, but I couldn't help but ask.

Paul continued to watch the screen and murmured, "It takes practice," just as a woman's voice with a trace of a Scottish accent said, "Hello?"

A round face with shortish dark hair appeared on screen, smiling. It was a moment before I could smile back: I couldn't see her aura. A question I'd have to bookmark for later. Maybe it was technology: the limitations of what can be detected and transmitted by a camera.

"Hi," Paul and I both said at once. I looked at him, letting him take the lead. As he quickly reiterated what I imagined he'd already told her by phone, I tucked my legs under me to one side. So, here I was, a part of their secret world. Should I feel guilty about it? I was unsure what to think.

"I'm Mel," the woman said, and I suddenly felt myself relax a little. "I'm very sorry to hear about the way in which you were Intrigued into this." That word again. So that was an actual thing, what Dale did to me?

"I definitely never meant to intrude," I said.

"Oh goodness, no," Mel said, and even Paul let out an indecipherable murmur next to me, sitting forward on the bench. "You mustn't think like that. After all, the other plane is a universal place – or is the gateway to one. It's just that the way we'd normally *invite* people to join our effort is with openness and choice. It's usually for people who have gone through great hardship and come out the other side. Often, they're already looking for ways to help others, get charity work and so on. But I'm getting side-tracked…"

Mel glanced away from the camera, biting her lip. Did she have a list of things to do or say? I blinked, closed my eyes for a second, but got a jump as I saw that goblin-creature staring at me again through my mind's eye. But this time a part of me wanted to stare back – to *do* something. As nightmarish as all of this was, it had the feeling of a war; something bigger than me, more important than just my own little life. I had a duty now, didn't I?

"I'll do the best I can. Just tell me what I need to do."

Mel beamed. "That's the spirit."

She got me to meditate. While Mel guided me through it, I sensed Paul settling into it too, which for some reason helped. Hearing his breath slow made me slightly calmer. Like a crest of a gentle wave, rising and falling. I was a tiny boat in an endless sea, but these two lovely people were with me. They were warriors, so much better than me. I wasn't worthy of any of this. My eyes began to sting, and I blinked them open. Paul's aura nearly made me gasp. It was the brightest gold, so bright I had to close my eyes again. Oh my God. Was that happening to me? Or could it happen, if I concentrated hard enough?

"What do you feel?" Mel had been asking me this from time to time throughout the breathing exercises. Sometimes I thought she was encouraging me to 'blank out' and feel nothing, other times she asked me to hone in on specific emotions. I imagined her leaning over me with a doctor's concerned frown, prodding my skin as if she were testing a rash.

"I'm just... a bit overwhelmed, that's all." My voice cracked. "Sorry."

"No apologies please. I just need you to be honest. Now, place your hand over the centre of your ribcage and press lightly. What do you feel?"

I felt like I'd found a button that would make me cry. "Like this is the centre where all my emotion gathers in one place?" Despite the audible tightness of my throat, my surprise broke through.

"Describe it. Use colours or shapes, whatever comes to you."

"Er." I pressed it again, but had to stop, it was too much. "Like a purple dot, or a blob. Or a bruise. It really is like a bruise…"

"OK. Just let it be. It's there in your chest, and it's there for a reason, okay? Fear and grieving, fear and grieving… They are physical sensations now. They are rooted in your chest, in your body. We're going to leave those behind."

We are?

"We're going to be working with higher vibrations now, when your mind joins the crow's. Only a part of your mind is to move with Sibelius, okay? The part that is open to hope and love. And by feeling hope and love, we can project those forces. To do this is we must observe the sensations in our bodies and choose to *leave the fear and grief behind.*"

Something clicked in my head. I knew I was supposed to be concentrating, but: was this why I fell, before? Was this why the goblin 'got me', because I'd gone up there full to the brim of my own fear? But look at me, I was holding my breath – that was no good. I exhaled slowly, counted myself back into the breathing rhythm Mel had taught me. This was going to be even harder than I thought, if I had to actually control my emotions and split my mind in two.

"How…" I began.

"Sense the golden glow around you. It is in the air. It is a part of you, but it is out there in the world. It is the part of you that is out there in the world. It connects you, makes you bigger. Feel yourself expand into the golden light."

As if this were a cue, next to me Paul whispered, "Bartok! Sibelius!"

The flapping of wings fanned the skin on my arms and face, and I ducked instinctively.

Paul murmured through a smile I could hear through his mask, "They won't poop on you."

Was I allowed to open my eyes? Paul had, though his eyes stayed heavy-lidded. The two crows were there in front of us, hobbling around the grass, pecking and turning their curious heads this way and that. It seemed like they were actually checking me out, in a friendly sort of way. How much could they understand?

But on the laptop screen, Mel's eyes were still closed. For a flash moment I wished I'd grabbed a cushion or something, it was getting uncomfortable sitting like this on the path, but there was no way I dared interrupt this state of mind, or whatever it was. I felt different after the meditation. Maybe it was to do with 'accepting' my emotions like that. Even the garden looked different. Everything seemed more alive. Colours thrummed as if the sun were out, but for now it was hidden behind bunched clouds. Hazily, a part of me hoped it wasn't going to rain and ruin my laptop, but the thought seemed far away, as if somebody else was thinking it; or like it was something I'd thought long ago, when I was a different person.

Mel began to sing. Her smooth, wavering voice rose up, not at all tinny through the laptop's speaker. This was bigger than technology, than pieces of plastic and metal welded together. An ancient folk song poured from her, the notes rising strong and heavy like a wave in a whale-filled sea.

It wasn't a language I recognised. It might not have been any language at all: perhaps these were chants, meant to loosen our ties to the petty meanings of this world, and pull us into the wordless understanding of the other one. That's what it felt like: an ancient magic, lifting me up. Mel paused to take a breath, and I imagined she was drawing on something deep within her, or maybe outside of her. That's what this was all about, wasn't it? The inside outside. The outside in.

But all I knew was, I wanted to ride those notes. The melody roved up and down, and I was riding over the ocean, no longer a boat but a thing of the air, winged and glorious. What? I didn't use words like 'glorious'. I had to see where this took me.

I opened my eyes just a slit to see both crows bowing to the song, spreading their wings with their beaks buried into the grass. I'd never seen a bird do that before. Were they in a trance? Were they obeying some command that was wrapped up in the song, the wavering, rising, falling song?

I closed my eyes again. *Expand into the golden light.* And I felt it. It was there, tingling on my skin. My grief and fear were just a speck now, buried deep in my chest, and the rest of me was spreading outwards beyond my skin. Those questions and doubts were behind me now. I could see: with my eyes closed, I could see. The garden looked different, though. I was closer to the ground, and the laptop was somewhere to one side.

Grass stems, sharp and intense, are spiked near my eyes. There is no danger, though. I am glorious. Tiny bugs crawl along the stems or in between them; I can feel-see them scratching, asking to be eaten. But I have no need of them right now. Not when the human leader sings the call-up song. That is when a human must ride.

Where is the tall one that works the garden? It is strange that he's gone. But this other human is the new one. The leader must want me to carry her, for now.

Those humans are such big ugly lumps, so unfortunate. Their minds are always trying to separate 'this' or 'that'. But they should know that all is everywhere. I'll show them. I'll show this new one how clever I am and how glorious.

Was I hearing the crow's thoughts? Almost. They had to be my own language-interpretation of his thoughts. So strange.

But as I stared around – as we, Sibelius and I, looked around us, his calm whirling around my terrified curiosity – there were other words, my words, getting tangled into the mix. Had I been thinking about 'ghost layers' earlier? Because I'd had no clue what that meant until now.

Wisps moved around us, superimposed on… reality. There was no other way to understand it. Shadow-people made from pale light or perhaps cloud, shifted like photo negatives over the air. Eyes turned and stared; a woman in a long cloak smiled beatifically, letting her ghost-hood drop before she turned to continue her graceful pacing. What looked to me like Indian gods and mythical forest creatures, centaurs and elves, old men with long beards, women with swollen bellies, danced or laughed or… made shoes? These were the beings of dreams, surely. Of a fairy tale realm. This had to be some hallucinogenic trick, although I'd done nothing to make this happen except meditate and listen to a song. All I'd had that day since breakfast was some water, nothing Paul could have tampered with – and why would he?

The song continued, Mel's voice seeming to both guide and calm me as I took in this new layer of perception. Paul's warning echoed back: don't focus too long on the shapes of thought.

I could feel Sibelius' sniggering attitude at my shock. It was a tangible sensation, his mind sitting side by side with mine. Smug self-satisfaction squashed up next to frightened awe. What a strong character, for a little bird! *Okay, okay. Not so little. 'Glorious', even.* At least he took his time, letting me pore over these phantasms long enough to become a little less afraid of them.

Vapours licked at the ghosts' edges. I saw the trees and even the gravestones through the places where their body-images thinned, as if my world was the unreal one, just a memory or a faded backdrop to their living play.

I didn't dare open my human eyes. Surely I would lose this new 'sight' in an instant if I did; this vision shared with me by a crow.

Mel's voice stopped. I was almost shocked that all the images didn't instantly disappear as the song ended, even as her talking voice, so ordinary, broke through the eerie atmosphere. "Turn your attention upwards."

Did she mean physically, or in the spiritual sense? Probably both. That's how it always was for spiritual people: metaphor and grand truths were hidden in everything like a second layer. And now, as a Watcher – if that's what I really was – I'd seen the truth, and it wasn't really a metaphor at all. It was right here around me, in these strange, dancing layers.

Mel added, "Turn your *thoughts* upwards. Sibelius will follow your directions now."

Really? I thought 'Up' and began to rise. A vague, black flapping showed in my peripheral vision, but I didn't dare let myself be distracted, not as we rose over the garden into the air. It was amazing, being able to fly. *OK, Sibelius, I agree with you. You are very clever.*

But were these clouds above us, or more ghosts? Everywhere I looked there were banks of vapour with nothing solid behind them. It was hard to understand what belonged to the normal world or the other plane when everything was layered like this. I had a feeling it was only going to get harder.

"Cast your heart outwards and upwards. Your compassion reaches. Your love and your hope, they reach. With your compassion you will see the golden light of love."

Woah. That sounded seriously trippy, but in the context, it made a kind of sense for what we were trying to do; what I was looking for. The light of love and hope, and the protective membrane that it helped to heal and guard. Not that I could see anything but clouds and other crows swooping about on silent wings, hey – other Watchers! – and... a dark gathering. Oh no.

It was worse than I remembered. The cloud actually hung lower at its darkest swell, as if struggling to contain the weight of all those jumbled creatures. Just as before, only there had to be more huddled in there this time. Elbows and feet peeked out, the promise of the rest of them: leathery wings and knuckled heads.

Just being near the heavy swathe, my veins were full of needles. I was sweating pin-pricks, the poison of fear flowing freely under my skin.

Sibelius shuddered, flapping unevenly in the air. I was freaking him out. *Stay calm, stay calm,* he thought. But how could I? Those things were going to come out any minute now – that's why we were here, right? Not that I understood what we were supposed to do when they did.

My mouth felt dry, and I tried to swallow. Just thinking about my human body threw my attention back down to it, but a part of me was still out there – or was it 'here'? – with Sibelius, feeling the air ripple through his feathers.

Sibelius looked down pointedly at the vague shapes in the garden, as if to prove the separation. In between the thought-ghosts I saw my body from above, more hunched than I'd thought, leaning forward as if I were trying to see something on the laptop screen, Paul's body next to me on the bench. So weird, to be in two places at once.

All is part of everything.

'Thanks for reminding me, Sibelius. Although I'm not sure that's going to help me face those things that are about to burst out of that cloud.'

Think *about what you can see up here! You humans have a ghost shape for everything, every part of who you are or who you might be. In this space of mind, all is potential. All things and beings in idea form;* ready-to-be *form. Look, here is bravery.*

Sibelius' thoughts seemed to point to next to us, as if a ghost were floating up with us. *I can't see anything,* I thought back to him.

Imagine, he seemed to say. The words 'think' and 'feel' were implied too, in the way he 'said' it.

Didn't Paul warn against focussing on the thought-shapes? But if I was creating one of my own, that was different, right? That couldn't really hurt, could it? If it gave me the courage I needed…

Your thoughts are your own. It's not every day you get to see them.

What was courage? I tried to imagine the feeling, and immediately realised it was less of an emotion than a decision you made. Courage was a thing you did in spite of what you felt. But what did that look like?

As if I had painted her myself using cloud vapour instead of paint, a figure appeared, hovering next to us. It – she – was somewhere between two- and three-dimensional; it was confusing to look at her, as her curls and wisps withdrew, flat, then moved and shifted around, making her seem on and off like a living, airborne sculpture. Her facial expression was strained but set as her eyes grew hard on something in the distance, something beyond me. Did she even see me? She was a figment of my imagination, wasn't she? So I saw her and not the other way round... right?

I looked down and saw that she wore a nurse's uniform. The appropriateness of that fact struck me nearly off balance, Sibelius' wings labouring as my breath caught in my 'real' throat below in the garden. She was a warrior, alright. A modern warrior, facing down death itself. She put her own life at risk, on the front line, to save other people's.

I needed some of that essence. That bracing quality, to do what I could. I might not be in a hospital fighting COVID-19, but there was a battle brewing here on a big scale – something that affected other people's wellbeing. I was worse than useless if I didn't have the guts to stay inside this crow and face those evil things.

The cloud-nurse took a step forward, pulling a mask up over her mouth and nose, and disappeared. In her place stood a young boy, staring at me.

Kyle?

Sibelius' wings *swicked* heavily in frustration, trying to shake me out of my state of mute shock.

No! This is too much like giving in to it, the crow was thinking. As his wings worked, he was drawing us away and to the side, away from this thought I'd had. Because it wasn't really Kyle; it was my idea of Kyle.

This isn't bravery, is it? I thought back weakly.

Black wings surged around me. We were a group of – how many? A dozen? Maybe twenty or thirty crows stirred the air with anticipation. I sensed unspoken, friendly caws from other crows, a part of the bigger 'we' that Sibelius and I were in. This wasn't a place where you cawed out loud, because of the danger that slithered and crept above us in the clouds – a threatening presence that I knew was there without glancing up. And as much as we didn't caw or make unnecessary noise or movement, neither did we stop dead in the air to stare at a ghost; certainly not a thought-shape that inspired our personal, Earth-bound fears.

We were a group. We were a 'we'. This was why you had to leave your grief and fear behind in your human chest.

One crow whipped past us in a confusion of black feathers: a warning, trying to shake me out of this. It was Mel's mind, riding one of these crows. Of course, the singing had stopped ages ago. Her voice beat at me softly inside my head, a disjointed sound. "Fear is a magnet. This is not the place to feel it. Train your thoughts back to the golden glow."

What golden glow? I no longer had the sense of it, that feeling I'd rose up with.

I was stalling now. Avoiding looking up at those creatures which I had to face. We all had to. I knew the others would protect me, but I still felt ill at the thought.

Mel 'spoke' again. "Look up! Look above you! *All hold positions!*"

This last command was clearly directed at everyone: a living, breathing army of crows, or minds-in-crows.

The goblins were out. They'd seen us.

Fear was an ugly crowd, and it was coming to get me. Poking elbows, sneering faces. Slithery leaden skin. Eyes like little beads of greed. Their hunger tugged at me, as if they'd latched on to flailing ribbon of weakness inside me and were pulling, pulling me towards their open mouths. Gas reeked, uncurling out from their pointed tongues. It was the smoke of a hundred snuffed candles, a hundred lives lost, souls plunged into nothingness.

They stank of toxic despair, a bile that lined the inside of my mouth – no, my beak. Wait, what was I? Where was our 'we'? I turned about, pumping my wings. It didn't feel the same, not as graceful as before, and as I turned to check Sibelius' wing, I lurched sideways in an unplanned move that had my/his stomach plummeting. There was something lopsided and difficult about the way I was flying. It was like trying to swim through treacle but heavier on my right-hand side. I expected a snide comment from Sibelius, but where his attitude 'was' before, there was nothing, just a weird sort of white hole. Vulnerability.

One of the goblins was plummeting towards me, a horrible grin opening its black-tongued mouth.

"Fear attracts Fear!" Mel's thoughts rang throughout my sickened, shivering body as I twisted away. "Use your compassion. Feel hope. You can help Kyle, and others like him – you must decide to!"

Another inner cry echoed right across the group, wordless this time. I recognised it instinctively, or perhaps through Sibelius' perception, as the highest type of command: the thing we were meant to do. Above me, gold light blasted. So beautiful. Beyond me.

I floated through the air, sensing Sibelius' surge of irritation at me – I was loosening from his host-mind, I was caught between two places.

Both at once! All is everything, he seemed to shout inside my head, but the stroke of leathery wings ruffled our feathers. The very air repulsed me. I couldn't do this 'golden light' thing – I didn't know how. Hope seemed impossible. Did they just think I would pick it up naturally, by watching the others?

I screamed as claws dug into my flesh. I was pulled through something, through a skin-like layer that stretched as my too-thick body was dragged through. I heard or felt a low pop over my head.

Golden light flashed again, but the rays missed me. I was there, back on the ground, in the garden. Opening my eyes. On the laptop screen, Mel was frowning, her eyes screwed up in concentration, her mouth open with the urgency to shout something. Paul sat forward on the bench, his fists clenched. Under closed lids his eyes seemed to search for something. A battle I couldn't see.

Sibelius fluttered down from the sky and landed on my lap, squawking at me.

"I'm sorry," I whispered out loud. "I don't know what happened there. It's all a bit much to take in."

He barked again and nosed off, pecking at the grass angrily like he didn't want to look at me.

The next few minutes were horrible. The feeling of having let them down, having made things quite possibly worse up there, churned inside my gut. Suddenly I wanted more than anything to be part of it and to make things right. Why shouldn't I fight alongside them? *Give me time to learn, and I'll work it out,* I silently begged Mel and Paul. But their minds were far away. Their eyes shut, both of them were fully occupied with their task, a spiritual duty they'd committed themselves to. Truly, I admired them. Yes, this was a *real* way to be; forget puny ambitions like having a good job and a shiny car, or even wanting to be a famous artist. What the Watchers did was vital for the human race.

The more I considered how incredible these people were and how meaningful their lives were, the less and less I thought of myself.

I couldn't sit here anymore. Now that I was fully 'in' my body, my leg muscles screamed at me to stand up. Stiff and not wanting to make a noise on the gravelly path, I leaned onto the grass and unfolded my legs. In between his pecking, Sibelius glanced my way although he had nothing but haughty looks for me. So peculiar, to know what it was like to be inside his mind and understand his funny attitudes and irritability – I almost smiled.

How long would Mel and Paul be? My stomach growled. Sarah's shopping sat untouched by the door to the church hall. There was probably milk and cheese in there, busy going off. As I debated in my head how long I could leave it before unpacking it and making an unforgivable noise, I paced gently, stretching out my legs and trying to work through my apology for when Mel and Paul came back 'down'. But was any of it really my fault?

Walking further up the garden, I couldn't help but glance at the tree where the gargoyle sat.

It wasn't there.

How could it not be there? We were the only ones in the garden. I put it there myself when Sarah arrived! And then I had walked away. I crept closer, my breathing shallow and quick. No. It had to have fallen off.

Nothing. There was no sign of it on the ground. I checked all the way around the tree.

It made no sense. What did it mean?

The next ten minutes were torture. I paced as quietly as I could, constantly glancing between the tree and Paul's face, for a sign that the Watchers were nearly done. Even Sibelius' curiosity overtook his decision to ignore me, and he began poking the ground around the tree, turning his eye my way as if asking what I was looking for.

Finally, Paul opened his eyes, frowning at where I stood. "Elina?"

"The gargoyle. It's gone!" Inside my head was white noise. All the words I didn't dare think came tumbling out. "Do you think it's possible I was inside it again, for a few seconds? Something happened up there. For a few seconds I was – lopsided, struggling to fly. It was when one of those *things* grabbed me and started pulling. But then why would it just disappear?"

Paul stood up and marched over, his stare fixed on the gap in the tree.

Silence. *Please, Paul, say something.*

He took out his mobile phone. He was flipping through screens, finding *redial*. Of course. Kyle's mother.

"Hello? Mrs Wells? It's Paul at the church. Yes, I – what's that?"

I was frozen. I was numb, watching Paul's face take on all the wrong expressions. His aura swarmed dark blue. I couldn't listen to the words that made no sense, the words that were reactions around an unheard, unspoken thing.

Eventually, the phone call was over, though it probably took less than thirty seconds.

Paul didn't look at me, but stared at my stomach instead. "Kyle has... run off."

No. I couldn't even think it, what this might mean, though the idea was already there, thumping like poison through my veins. "We have to go and look for him. Where was he when – ?"

Now Paul was looking at me. "Elina. You have to stay here. You're self-isolating, remember?"

Oh yes. That thing. I was most likely infected with a deadly disease... but that seemed less worrying now that...

"It's something I did, isn't it? The gargoyle's connected to Kyle's mind... Oh God, what have I done? Will he be alright?"

"Stay here," was all he said, and strode off to speak to Mel through the laptop.

So much fear. How was there space in my body for all of this? While Paul was out with Mrs Wells looking for her son, I waited in the garden on my own, stewing in my own terror. Thick ribbons of coldness flashed through me, twisting to reveal heat on their undersides. Heat? Really? Was I angry, on top of everything else?

It hit me like a fist, like the taste of blood in my mouth. *Dale.* This was all his fault. He'd forced me into this situation, he'd 'Intrigued' me with his messed-up letter. The scheming bastard wanted out, and threw me into this instead. He knew my connection to the kids, to the craft group! Not that he could've known this would happen, but still. I'd been thrown headfirst into this situation without a clue, without a chance, and now a boy's *life* might hang in the balance...

It was too much. I was shaking now. I couldn't sit here anymore, useless, waiting. I had to go and speak to Dale. I would tell him what he'd done. Yes, what *he* had done. But I didn't know where he lived. Paul had a contact list, but I wasn't prepared to add breaking-and-entering to my sins. I'd done enough damage today without adding actual crimes to the agenda.

Sibelius cocked his head at me as if trying to listen to my thoughts.

"Sibelius. You know where Dale lives."

I'd been in the crow's mind once before, hadn't I?

Part 4

The Other Side

Sibelius bowed, his black wings touching their soft finger ends against the grass. I sat with my back against the tree trunk and began humming, trying to recall some echo of Mel's tune. Sibelius twisted round to throw me a quizzical glare that seemed to say, 'Not *now*, stupid,' so I settled back and closed my eyes. Was this enough? Could we just do this again by willing it? Perhaps the trance-like state was still fresh enough in my mind, because within seconds I was back inside the crow, gliding over suburbia.

Rooftops and rectangles of green swooped underneath us. From this angle, the streets seemed like a never-ending pattern of roads, intersections, and box-like houses. It was as if, as a species, we were so desperate to prove that we controlled and ordered life itself that we'd ended up trapping ourselves in this sprawling, jumbled prison of concrete and brick. These might have been the crow's thoughts rather than my own, but for a little while I let them course through me, a pleasant distraction from my swirling, hot-blooded mood. After all, it hardly mattered whose thoughts they were.

It matters, thought Sibelius. A mental image flashed before us: a young woman's face, unfamiliar. She sat with her eyes closed and her head tipped against the back of a chair while people gathered around her trying to shake her awake. Outside this scene, a crow, slightly smaller than Sibelius, wheeled in the air, cawing harshly.

Mentally I took in a breath. 'You can get stuck like this?'

It's worse for the crow host.

'Don't worry, I'm not planning to bug you forever. I just need to see where Dale's place is.'

At the thought of Dale, a fresh wave of anger surged through me, colouring the landscape once more. But it had a weird aftertaste, like the feeling had an underside: Sibelius' reluctance beat heavy as his wings, weighing him down. Us.

Calm down. Please. Your anger is uncomfortable. You're not the only one here.

'Show me where Dale lives and I'll get out of your hair – feathers – whatever. I'll come back in my human form to confront him. Then I'll feel better.'

But would I? And how would that help Kyle? Could anything help him now, or undo what I'd done – whatever that turned out to be?

As I scrutinised the twisting streets, it seemed like there was no end to my feelings, these swathes of fury and frustration that might have been stripes of red. They reached... everywhere. I could turn my gaze to a windowsill, a street light, a post box, and each one quivered as if I might make it come alive or else make it shrink with the sheer force of my glare.

We were wheeling again, dawdling in circles over the rooftops.

'Sibelius! I'm not coming out of you until you show me where Dale lives. Look, all I want to do is talk to him, okay?'

We flew on in silence and finally Sibelius' attention seemed to fix on a particular spot. There: an end of terrace house with a wooden gate at the front and a neatly clipped hedge. *Naturally. He's a gardener, you know.*

'Thanks – I appreciate it. Now, please let's go back in a straight line so I can find my way back here on foot? Do you think you could manage that? You know, "*as the crow flies*"?'

Flying back, in between studiously tracing the cross-sections and turns and notable landmarks, a delicious, tickly sensation rippled through my gut. Not my gut, but the crow's. Sensing my curiosity, Sibelius repeated my own thoughts back to me with all the sarcasm he could muster: *As the crow flies?*

Of all the weird and crazy things that had happened over the last day and a half, to discover that crows have a sense of humour…

Back inside my human body, I grabbed a bottle of hand sanitizer from Sarah's shopping, then quickly dumped the bag inside the church hall and threw the perishables into the fridge. Why should my cheese and milk go off, on top of everything else? Some part of me was still hoping for a return of normal life after all this. But would it?

No time to think about it: just before the gate, I gasped to see the gargoyle lying on the ground, half hidden by a bush. But why shouldn't it drop down in a slightly different place? It was hardly miles away. I hesitated before I picked it up, cupping the broken wing against its body, making my mind up to take it with me. It felt like evidence; proof of what Dale had caused me to do.

It must have been about a ten-minute walk to his house although it felt much longer. Everything looked different at ground level, and I realised I was using crow-based thinking to find my way, like distinctive trees and clusters of chimney pots which I couldn't see properly from here. I retraced my steps and refocussed on the general directions of the roads.

At the sight of the wooden gate, fresh anger stabbed my chest. I slowed, trying to catch my breath. I'd been striding, full of balled-up frustration, and the face mask was hot and stuffy.

I stopped, tucked the gargoyle under my arm and rubbed alcohol gel over my hands before opening the gate. I might be livid, but I was still in control. Ignoring the shake of my hands and the fact I had no idea what I might say when I saw Dale, I pressed the doorbell twice then took two strides back.

The door opened. Dale's pale face emerged from the gap, frowning vaguely as if he couldn't – or didn't dare – believe that I was real. "Hello?"

But despite his apparent dullness, I realised with a quick in-breath that I'd never really *seen* Dale before. His aura's bubble churned vividly, a giant purple bruise. Directly over his chest was a gaping hole, like something torn open. What did that mean?

Who cares?

"You owe me, Dale. You owe me an explanation." I was pointing at him now. I've always hated it when people point, but here I was, jabbing my finger like I wanted to poke another hole in his aura, the anger rising liquid and bloody inside me. I imagined ripping off my mask and standing closer, giving him a little more than he deserved.

I stayed where I was. Dale said nothing. He seemed dumbstruck, or unable to process the fact that I was here.

The mask against my hot skin was another layer of infuriation, shuffled and piled on top of all the others – itches I couldn't scratch. Yet it was tears that threatened to break through as I accused him. "You landed me in this, Dale... You threw me in the deep end, and now I can't close my eyes. I can't ever close my eyes again."

I pinched my eyes shut anyway, inwardly staring back at the evil face that pierced me from the other side. "And now Kyle," I added, my voice cracking.

"Kyle?" he bleated back at me, stupidly.

"Yes, Kyle. That's his name, by the way. The boy who made this gargoyle!" I shook it at him.

Dale's eyes slid to the lifeless clay model and back to my face again, narrowing at me as if trying to see past this weird new nonsense about gargoyles so he could work out what was 'really' going on with me.

"You reached too far," he said in his bland voice, like a statement and a question in one. He was asking me to confirm it, while he watched me with that careful, all-knowing way – as if he knew me completely, and that I should just accept my own short fallings.

Oh, so it was my fault. I'd simply 'reached too far'.

My breath was hitching as I prepared to tell him exactly what happened and whose fault it was.

But before I could, Dale opened his hands as if presenting a reasonable argument. "Sorry, but second-generation Watchers never get it right."

"*What?*" I spluttered. This new idea rushed like cold water through all my insides. No – no way could it be true! So why did Paul and Mel bother trying to teach me, if that were the case? Not that they seemed that surprised when things went wrong. Dismayed, yes. But not surprised.

A new heat flashed my cheeks. "So you *knew*… You knew this, and you did it anyway. You set me up for failure. How could you?"

He wagged his head as if a great weight was bearing down on him, and he could only move and think in slow motion. His voice was as bleak as his expression. "I'm sorry I had to pull you into this, but however bad it is for you, for me, it's unworkable. I've no hope left to give. Sibelius would've latched on to someone of his own accord. It was better for me to make sure he chose someone young, and strong."

Strong? Had I mentioned my likely COVID infection to Dale? I couldn't even remember, but it hardly mattered.

"Do you want to know what I did?" I pulled myself up taller, quivering with rage. "I flew inside this gargoyle. Not Sibelius, but a dead clay model, made by Kyle. A *vulnerable child* who has a tough home life. I broke its wing, see? Those *creatures* broke its wing, and now Kyle's missing. I don't even know what I've done." It was too much. I hunched over with the effort of saying it; the effort of not hitting him, not shaking him, whilst saying it. "And you. It's your fault. You made me. Do this."

Dale stood there empty-eyed as a ghost. Like a figure that should have been made of cloud but was somehow, eerily, real.

"I'm sorry." His voice seemed far away. "I couldn't have known. I saw an opening – I saw your fear, and – "

Behind me the wooden gate began to rattle. I paused before I turned, flushed, expecting to see a delivery person with a package ducking their head in embarrassment, or a dog walker tugging at the leash while their dog refused to pull away from this gate post – the one gate post in the whole street where they really shouldn't linger because two people were having a full-blown argument in the front yard. But there was no-one. Just a gate shuddering on its hinges.

"Please step aside," Dale murmured. He strode past me and clamped both hands down on the gate, his head bowed as if braced against something.

"What the – ?"

"You're going to have to calm down," he said so quietly I wasn't sure if I'd misheard. "I know you're angry, and I'm very sorry for what's happened, but you have to calm down or things will get out of control."

There was a slight movement to my right, so quiet that in any other circumstances I wouldn't have bothered looking, believing it must be some dry leaves dragged by the wind. But Dale jerked round as if by instinct. Still leaning his weight on the shuddering gate, he reached out and caught the rim of the bucket as it flew into his open hand.

I had a flashback of Dale standing there in the church hall gardens, eyes peering at me in the semi-dark, his hand tight around his spade. He hadn't loosened his grip on that spade, even when I thought he might shake my hand, until he'd marched some distance past me on his way to fetch Paul, when he'd rested it carefully against the shed. It was just a detail, one of many creepy-seeming details at the time, but I'd been so freaked out to start with that I'd thought nothing more of it.

Seeing Dale now in broad daylight, cringing against the gate with his arm muscles thickening under his shirt, it all came together. This was Dale's secret; this was the reason he was so quiet and spent hours longer than was needed in the church hall gardens. I'd thought him slow, or deeply troubled. Well, he was that.

He made objects move. Quite random objects. Or were they?

His voice was still dull but a little friendlier as he said it. "Let's continue this conversation in the back garden, shall we?"

I followed him at a distance, throwing one last glance back at the gate. If it was still trembling, it was imperceptible from here. Dale strode ahead like he never wanted to look at it again. Perhaps this was a tactic. If some objects were 'sympathetic' towards him, he could lessen the effect by walking away or switching his attention to something else. Was that how it worked? My mind buzzed with possibilities as I trailed after him along the side of his house into a broad, beautifully kept garden edged by large trees.

My phone was a large, uncomfortable shape in my pocket. Every second that it didn't ring, Kyle was still lost and Paul was out looking for him with Mrs Wells. But this, with Dale, was at least a distraction from the oil slick of worry that swilled in my gut. And I was going to learn something from Dale; he had no reason to hold things back from me, like Paul and Mel had. My chest fluttered to think it, but here was another 'second-generation' Watcher who might make sense of this whole mess…

One step at a time.

"Okay, first, you're going to tell me: why. Why does it never work with second-generation…?" It sounded wrong to me the moment I said it out loud, and I didn't want to finish the sentence. I also didn't feel like sitting on the lawn with this guy as if we were here to have a little picnic and a nice chat, but what else was I going to do? "And I take it that Paul and Mel are first-generation?"

Dale sat a few metres away from me, staring at his grubby trainers. He blinked slowly, as if it hurt to bring up this knowledge from somewhere deep inside him. As he spoke, his aura blushed patches of a lighter, cornflower blue.

"As a Watcher, you have to be strict with your emotions. You have to keep something behind, to anchor your body in this place," he pointed at the ground, "and that's always the darker stuff. If you take it up with you, you'll only draw *them* closer." I knew he had to mean those creatures.

"Love must be pure," he continued. "The healing force," he added with a low chuckle, although it came out with a rasping catch in his throat. "When Kate died, *love* meant I was all over the place."

"Kate?" Inwardly, I scrambled for the memory of someone called Kate and found no-one. "Was she your…"

"Wife, yes. I don't suppose I ever told you about her, did I?" He turned away to quickly wipe his nose. "She died of Alzheimer's. Towards the end, she didn't even know who I was." He was looking down the whole time he spoke. When a tear slid off the side of his nose, I realised why.

"After that, I couldn't stop looking for her in the clouds. I found her, a ghost in the sky. But it wasn't her. How could it be? It was too cruel, to see her that way: nothing but a thought, a memory. Never *her*. It was too much.

"But then I began to lose my connection to Sibelius. When I say I was all over the place, I mean that literally. My feelings… were scattered. They got into things. Well, mostly gardening tools. Things that are bound up with memory, of times spent with Kate. She was a landscape gardener, you know, much fancier than me." He smiled a small smile. "Those poor other crows and Watchers had to duck whenever my spade slipped through, or that bloody bucket. I was feeling too many things at once, latching on to things at random. And love…" He exhaled, piecing his way slowly through words like stepping stones over rushing water. "My love for Kate was also my pain. My love was also my *fear*, because I thought I'd be trapped like this, in grief, for the rest of my life."

I paused. What were you supposed to say to something like that? "I'm really sorry, Dale. That's really rough... just awful. But please keep going. Tell me rest. So you were making objects... not come alive, I assume? Just move?"

"It was out of control. But I'm not as bad now. What you saw..." He glanced at me, earnest now. "I managed to stop taking things up there with me, but they still shift about on this plane, when my emotions get out of hand. I can still ride Sibelius, but those creatures. They won't leave me alone."

I sat up straight. "Me too! The bit about creatures not leaving me alone, I mean. Not the rest, obviously..."

Despite my determination to stay mad at him, I was softening towards Dale and beginning to understand him a little bit. Not that that made it all okay, though...

"I was half a Watcher, really," Dale said, shaking his head at the lawn. "Less than half. They've tolerated me long enough, even tried to counsel me." He raised his eyebrows and actually grinned at me. "It got dangerous."

"Seriously?" I found this weirdly impressive. "You do know that a comic book writer would go totally crazy with this right now?"

He laughed softly then paused, staring at the space between us. "Yeah. But what you need to know about second-generation Watchers is that there've been other problems."

I bristled at this but kept very still. "Like what?"

"Like, some of them got obsessed with the ghost-thoughts, couldn't tear themselves away. Or they'd get curious about what else is up there, thinking, 'What would happen if I passed through the membrane into the collective unconscious itself? What would I find?'"

My eyes were wide. "What would you find?"

"All sorts, good and bad. Purer forms of those ghost-thoughts. The basis of myth itself. Primal... knowledge? Huh, stuff that only makes sense in dreams."

"Wow."

"Don't even think about it." Dale looked at me sharply. "The dangers up there are more than any one person can handle. You could lose yourself, lose your hold on life. Think how easily you could get lost. I think that's why they use crows. You have to keep a careful separation."

"Oh my God. Sibelius just told me about someone who got lost up there..." I looked around half expecting to see the cheeky crow on the fence or the lawn, tilting his head at our conversation.

"What? Now?" Dale's head flicked round, searching with me. "Can you hear his thoughts right now?"

"Oh! *No.*" I almost laughed, then it struck me. "But that would be weird, wouldn't it?" Silently I added, 'and not necessarily impossible.' After all these failures and difficulties, things which Paul hadn't told me about – I guess he was in a rush to try and make it work rather than give me a potted history – who knew what we could actually do, if we experimented? Were our failures actually failures, or were they the potential new beginnings of... something else we could do?

My gaze caught on my jeans pocket, and my heart thudded in response. *Still* my phone hadn't rung! Had Paul forgotten me? Would he call me straight away when he found Kyle? Should I, could I, call him to check?

I let out a slow breath, hot under my mask. "So tell me. How did it start? With the 'first-generation'? Were they always perfect?"

"The Watchers were just a bunch of people meeting for prayer, to start with. Well, not necessarily prayer, because they're multi-faith and totally open, so some people prayed while others meditated or practised positive thinking. But they agreed on one thing: that when people put their energies together, something happens.

"I think they originally meant to meditate for calm and healing. They're all counsellors in one way or another, being spiritual leaders, and when you help people who are stressed out, some of that stress tends to rub off onto you. That can make it hard to keep going, on to the next person. I think that's where the idea came from, for splitting up your emotions and leaving your fear behind in your chest while your compassion reaches outwards. Well, there really is something about compassion that reaches." His mouth twitched. He was enjoying telling his story. "They reached further than they expected to; assisted by Mel's pet cockatiel and some flies or midges."

"What?" I choked on the word, almost laughing. This was too much; too bizarre.

"They told you about animals, didn't they? Seeing both planes at once?"

"Yes, but… Sorry, it just sounds so ridiculous. So makeshift. When Mel started humming that song, I honestly thought there was some grand old ancient tradition…"

"That's true. But everything is makeshift to start with. Even ancient traditions. So they glimpsed the other plane, but repeating the experience was harder to do. Squawky didn't really understand what her owner was trying to do, and the flies were just, well, flies."

Now I was laughing. "Go on," I managed.

With a flicker of a smile, Dale continued, setting his gaze on something far in the distance. "They tried other animals. Dogs were eager to please, but they didn't get it. While they see what other animals see, they're too human-oriented in their thinking, and distracted by this plane. Cats had no patience and wouldn't take directions. But since the group's new purpose was to explore *upwards* and revisit the dangers they'd only just glimpsed in the clouds, winged creatures were the obvious choice..."

My phone rang, sending a thrill right up the side of my body. My knees suddenly stiff, I staggered up, fumbling to get the damn thing out of my pocket.

"Hello?"

"Elina." Paul's voice, quiet and close. "False alarm." He added, much louder, "Kyle's fine – he just ran off into the woods while he was playing."

"But – really?" There was something overly bright and cheerful in his tone, like he was trying to cover up something. "Are you with him right now?"

"Yes, I'm with Kyle and Mrs Wells. Funny coincidence, that I just happened to ring Mrs Wells at that moment, and I suppose we fed off each other's panic. It took me a little while to find the place, and of course I wasn't going to use the phone while I was driving…"

The sweet flavour of relief filled me up. But still. What was Paul keeping from me? If I didn't ask now, I'd lose my chance. There was some vital piece of information here, I knew it – and Kyle might be the only one who'd tell me.

"Ohh, it's been so long since I've seen Kyle. Can I chat to him quickly? Please? Just put us on video chat, will you? Please Paul?"

I heard a sigh, then the call ended. I stood there staring at my phone, willing it to happen, until the invite button flashed up.

Paul's masked face frowned a warning at me before he turned aside.

"Look who wants to say hello to you, Kyle! It's Elina. Do you remember Elina? It was a couple of summers back." The image turned to a rush of pavement as Paul said, "No need to touch the phone, okay? I'll just rest it on this wall here. She can see you." Then louder, "Can you see him okay, Elina?"

Almost. "Can you shuffle to the left slightly? No, sorry, my left, your right. There you are! Hi, Kyle." I waved and pulled down my mask so he could see my face properly. "Remember me?"

Kyle eyed me shyly, though his frown began to clear as he checked me over. "I think so…"

"Look what I've got with me! It's your gargoyle, remember?" I picked it up, careful to train it at an angle so he couldn't see the broken-off wing.

He stared in amazement, grinning as he came closer to the screen. My heart squeezed: he was just the same sweet-faced boy, though his face was a little less round. "Oh yeah."

I didn't have much time. His mum was right there behind him, and it would probably seem a weird jump in the conversation, but I knew I couldn't rest unless I asked him – I knew I'd replay the same moment in my head all night, desperately imagining his answer.

"So what were you doing running off in the woods just now? What did you see?" I said, trying to keep my tone light, but my eyes meaningful so he might understand. But would he?

"Oh, nothing really. I was playing." He was so confident. Little Kyle was growing up; learning to lie so smoothly.

"Playing?" I laughed but it sounded false. "What were you playing? I miss playing pretend like I used to with my school friends," I added quickly. This had always been my tack with the kids. Talk at their level. I was the weirdo grown-up; they were the 'real' ones, who knew what life was really like.

With a slight giddiness, I realised this might be closer to the truth than I'd ever dreamed.

Kyle pouted over whether to tell me, and looked away, his face creased in an embarrassed smile. But Paul and Mrs Wells were talking softly behind him, distracted.

"Go on, you can tell me," I coaxed him. "I bet you could draw the most amazing picture of it – I'd love to see that. I remember how fantastic you are at drawing."

At this he nodded. Always, his artwork 'ruled'. "Umm, I saw something nasty, and I ran after it." He scrunched up his face in a thoughtful look. "Like a big evil goblin thing. But it was no match for me – hii-*ya!*" He struck out to the side in a martial arts move. Though he might have picked it up from a cartoon and was probably something he and his friends did all the time in the playground, inventing superhero identities for themselves, this simple action left me speechless. He saw one of those creatures, on this plane. He saw it and had no fear. That, or this truly was a game to him and he didn't believe it was real. Was there something magical in the make-believe play of children that helped them see things this way, protecting their minds?

I swallowed. "Wow. You showed him. So... have you played this before?

His dark eyes were bright with a stubborn fierceness. He grinned back. "Plenty, with my mates."

Oh God. It was nothing he hadn't seen before.

I could sense a strange silence emerging from the two adults behind him. I could just imagine how Paul's mind must be racing over this while he tried to make conversation with Mrs Wells, all the time wondering how far I was going to push it.

"So, Kyle, maybe some time when I'm – available to visit people, I could bring this back, would you like that?" I held the gargoyle up again.

Doubt crossed his face. "But it protects the forest." The brightness in his eyes clouded over; I didn't understand his games after all.

Raised murmurs in the background made him glance back to his mum; they had other places to be, and it was time to go. "See you, bye!" he said, and the image swerved back round to Paul as he picked up his phone again.

"See?" Paul said. "He's all fine. Better than fine. *I'll see you later*," he said, scrutinising my face, as if trying to work out what exactly what I was thinking.

"Oh my God," I said to Dale, slipping my phone back into my pocket. "Kyle's not hurt. But he saw one of those things, and he chased it off! He'd seen them before. How is any of this possible?"

"Children are different. Their view of the world is different. They see both planes."

"What? You mean like animals?" Another thing Paul hadn't told me. God, the amount of worry I could've saved myself had I known…

"Not quite, no. Animals can't see the distinction, it's all the same to them. With children, it's more like different layers they can zone in and out of, more or less at will. It all depends on their imaginations. Which children have bucket-loads of."

"I don't get it. Imagination? But this is *real*." I was pacing about on the grass while Dale just sat there, telling me these weird theories as if he'd read them in a text book years ago.

"Fantasy and reality are two sides of the same coin. This makes more sense when you're a child, when everything is new and weird. A stressed-out child will often use make-believe to work through their emotions, like playing. We forget a lot of this as we grow up. The only switch-back we get between realities is when we watch a film or read a book, and even then, it's more like a memory of an old skill. But we still have it: the meditation, how we enter the mind of the crow, that's all the work your imagination. Like, if you don't believe in it, it won't work. Imagination is why children are more resilient than adults, by the way. I'm not surprised Kyle is okay."

"What? Are you serious?"

Dale nodded. "Think about it. When kids are in trouble, they just keep going. Through play and pretend, they manage to keep going. It's usually in adulthood when childhood traumas come back to haunt us and we end up in therapy."

"But how come I don't remember... monsters in my childhood?"

He gave me a curious smile. "You'll forget what's convenient to forget. How many adults would function in the 'real' world if they still believed in monsters?"

I frowned at him, bemused. "This is something you've thought about a lot."

He shrugged, nodding. "Kids are cool. They're brave, but most adults can't see it."

"Wait, wait, hang on," I said, pulling out my phone again and holding it out. "The creature Kyle just ran after in the woods. Is Paul really saying it's just a coincidence? It just happened to turn up when I was inside Kyle's gargoyle?"

He frowned. "You were worried there's a link between Kyle and his gargoyle, which might've drawn a Fear-beast to him?" Dale stood up slowly, his eyes fixed on something past my shoulder. "I don't think so, because there's one behind you right now."

Impossible.

Sunk on its haunches in a predatory pose, a creature spread its long, curled fingers over the tiles on the roof, sniffing them. Its mottled, olive-grey skin winked in the uncertain March sunlight. Truly, a thing that didn't belong here in ordinary suburbia, overlooking a garden that burst with beauty and life.

And yet as its eyes hooked on mine, I knew that stress was a sickness inside my soul. There was nothing I could do to defend myself against that thing, because it *was* my own terror. All of the dread I'd ever felt, all the middle-of-the-night cold sweats; the emptiness that had lived at the core of my being so long it might as well be a bodily organ.

The creature's greasy skin slithered and stretched over sinew and bone as it leant forward to drink in the sight of me. I stood there, as if holding my ground, but useless. It wasn't just a beast; it was the knowledge that I was going to die. It pointed at my mask and snickered. My stomach roiled in response. Understanding puddled in my gut like poison: the creature was saying, 'sooner than later, my friend,' as clearly as Sibelius could speak inside my head.

How could I fight something that was as much inside me as it was in the outside world?

I had to try! I cast about for a weapon, though simply moving my neck brought a wave of nausea into my muscles. My body was in 'freeze' mode, a survival switch that wasn't any use to me here. *What about fight or flight? – Fight, definitely fight,* I thought wildly, bending to grab a trowel that stuck out of the flowerbed to my left. I held up the tool, waving it slightly, though my eyes were watering and my shoulders racked with shivers.

The beast sniggered and made a clucking noise deep in its throat – something I'd heard before, up in the clouds. Just the sound of it sent a part of me plunging through a sky I'd never leave behind, a powerlessness that was a part of me now.

Dale whispered from somewhere behind me, his voice seeming to evaporate. "The pandemic's changed everything. There's nowhere Fear won't go…"

"Pandemic? Or was it me, tearing a hole in the membrane?" Despite the horror of what I was admitting, speaking out loud broke a little of the spell and I waved my trowel back and forth in warning. Naming my terrors gave them a sense and a shape I could handle a little better – and any shape was more manageable than the one that hissed and spat right above me.

Dale was silent for a beat as he took in what I'd said. "Did you – ?" Shock cracked through his hushed tone like yolk from a broken egg.

"Maybe. I don't know! There was this popping sound as one of them pulled me *through*…"

Another silence from behind me.

"Okay, now is not the time to have an existential crisis," I said, trying to believe the new steadiness in my voice. "What am I supposed to…?"

The trowel was too short; I wanted to create distance between me and that thing. Anything that might wipe the stinking grin off its face – before it decided to breathe its God-awful dread. "Why does your garden have to be so bloody *neat?*"

A hose lay in a thickly coiled circle a short way to my right. Too heavy, too soft? But if I lassoed it a bit, it might cause enough of a sting to make the creature back off. I sidestepped away from the beast, though its piercing eyes followed my every move. Quickly, I grasped the end of the hose and unwound it a couple of metres.

"Don't!" cried Dale.

"Why?" I muttered, and flicked the hose back, swinging it like a whip. A quick side-slap and the creature hunched up protectively.

"You'll only make it stronger!"

"Doesn't look stronger to me," I said, but the goblin was scrunched up so hard its bones pushed against its skin as if they might split through. Surely my warning cuff wasn't enough to make the creature cower like this? But something was happening. Bones and muscle were creaking, snapping – growing. The thing was swelling in size. Its long fingers loosened and spread open to reveal claws twice the length. With a deep in-breath, the creature unfolded itself, arms outspread and head thrown back in a sort of victory stance. As the sun slid behind clouds then winked out again, the beast's skin shimmered. A strange murmur trembled in its throat as if it were chanting to itself and gathering strength to lash out.

"Dale, for God's sake!" I cried over my shoulder. "Where's that spade of yours? Where are your tools?"

"I told you. If you hurt it, it will get stronger!"

I turned to snatch a glance at him. "You know an awful lot, for someone who's basically given up."

"It's not enough to know," he said, sounding hollow. His arms sagged at his sides. "It's what you *do*."

"Then *do* something, won't you? Instead of just passing the buck?" Dale glanced up just as I threw him a meaningful look. *Yes, Dale. When you passed your Watcher-hood on to me, that's exactly what you were doing.*

But I was too busy with this creature to keep up an argument at the same time. I heard Dale huff behind me and… Did he just flop down on the grass?

"Get away from me!" I flicked the hose back and forth, not close enough to hit it again but to maintain a slight distance. Clearly it pained the thing to grow and swell like that, despite the advantage that it gave it.

What was I thinking? The creature had several advantages over me, without even trying. Already its tongue was lolling out between its front fangs. It drew a short, wheezy in-breaths, each one gathering in length. Oh no. Not the gas.

"Can't you do *anything?*" I cried over my shoulder at Dale. A seasoned Watcher, and all he could do was lie there sunbathing.

A movement on the ground near my foot caught my eye. The gargoyle hobbled along the grass looking like a strange, wind-up toy that should have been made from brightly coloured plastic, not dull clay. With a clumsy flap of its one and a quarter wings it half jumped, half swooped onto the drainpipe, crawling up. The Fear-beast's mean eyes narrowed at me as it snickered again. In a grin of delight, its black tongue slithered in and out, jaw widening with greed. Its stomach swelled as it inhaled. I was ready to run, but no way was I going to leave the gargoyle here to get smashed to pieces. Logic told me it was just a clay model, and the damage wouldn't hurt Kyle, but still it made no sense.

What was Dale going to do?

But as a fog of vile smoke blossomed around me like the breath of death itself, I spotted the little gargoyle clambering over the top of the guttering. It stuck out its short, wide tongue that looked dry in comparison to the beast's, just a stubby slab of clay – and breathed golden light. The goblin staggered back as if dizzy, its beady eyes rolling back, and promptly disappeared.

As the fog slowly cleared, I stood staring at the empty space on the roof where the thing had just been.

Behind me, Dale murmured, "Open your hands," just as the figurine stiffened and fell off the ledge. I reached for it and caught it, turning around.

"How – how did you just do that?"

Dale rubbed his eyes with his palms, sitting up. "I saw you talking to Kyle earlier; I heard his voice, got a sense of who he is."

"You got a sense…?"

He shook his head as if he was shaking off sleepiness, or the otherness of that other plane. "That's how you connect with an object, I guess. That's how you did it. And I meant to explain earlier. Love or compassion isn't just a feeling, it's a general attitude. It's something you decide to be."

My mind whirled with a dozen questions as I lay the gargoyle on the grass. What Dale just did. It meant something; something good. But the fog of dread was still too fresh within me to think clearly. A sickly shade of green pressed against the underside of my skin, and I clutched my arms, shivering.

It didn't help that Dale was in full-blown 'doom and gloom' mode. "This new Fear... with the coronavirus everywhere, it's too strong. Too widespread. The promise of death and grief. Even the prime minister says we will lose people. Thousands. There's no escape from that."

"It's the Watchers' job to keep Fear at bay!" I snapped back, feeling nothing of the anger I tried to throw at him. "Why do you have to be so negative? A minute ago, you were like, 'love is an attitude, love is a choice'. I just don't get you, Dale."

"We're not enough, that's all." Dale sank back down again on the grass, squeezing his eyes shut against the sun, or against any argument I could fling against him. "We're not enough."

"Then we can get more, train more people! Whatever you say about second-generation Watchers – there's stuff we can do that Paul's never even thought of. We move objects." I sat forward. "It means something. Something we can *use*. What you did with Kyle's gargoyle just then. You breathed love. Is that how it works with the crows? I've never quite seen what it is they do."

"No. With the crows it just glows around you – them." He swatted his hand lazily against the idea. But after a long silence, he seemed to notice I wasn't talking anymore, and he sat up, his forehead crossed with curiosity and irritation.

I was jiggling on the grass, struggling to contain my excitement. "You made it up. Just like the first Watchers made it up. And that weird poem you used to 'intrigue' me... It's imagination. Imagination is important." Despite my jelly legs, I was pacing again. "And now the gargoyle – sticking out its tongue like that. How did you know that would work?"

Dale scratched the side of his head. "I didn't. But that's what gargoyles normally do. They were designed to scare of evil spirits and would often have sticking-out tongues... What?"

I stood still, though my heart was jumping about like crazy. "Kyle gave it away. He *gave* it *away*." An idea buzzed in my head and in my fingertips.

"What are you thinking?"

I gestured with my hands. "Do you think it's significant that Kyle gave it away as a gift? The *intention* of it... He left it in the church gardens, in that tree. He said it was there to protect the forest. I mean, by 'forest', he was only being imaginative... But imagination, that's what we need! Kids have tons of it. What if we get others like Kyle to just 'give it away'? More clay models, with wings. With that get-back attitude. Then we can ride them all to hell..."

Dale's eyes widened, though he tilted his head away from me as if he didn't fancy looking at this idea head-on. "You mean...?"

But I had another question. "How many objects can you split your mind into at one time, if you concentrate enough?"

Dale's mouth wagged before he said anything. "I've never concentrated on it. It's something I try *not* to do."

"Okay, fine, but how many?"

He was quiet. "Four or five, on a bad day..."

"Four or five?" I cried, bouncing up and down. "But what if you tried? What if you actually put your mind to it – ha, literally! And could you teach me?"

He scrunched his forehead at me. "What are you thinking?"

"A whole fleet. A whole army of gargoyles. Just think of it."

"I don't... I don't see how. Paul would never agree to it."

"Well, maybe I'm not asking Paul's permission. Paul doesn't know everything, does he? He didn't know how to handle what was happening to you. The Watchers definitely need more manpower... womanpower..."

"Kidpower?" He rolled his eyes. "You can't be serious?"

"All we have to do is empathise with the kids that make them. You did it, just watching me talk to Kyle for five minutes.

"I'd have to do webinars. But then... how are we going to get the kids together online? We'd have to do it through their parents, and make sure they've got enough modelling clay." I sighed. "I can order clay online, that's the easy part. But gathering enough kids – the only way to do it quickly is to contact parents at the church. And that means going through Paul...

I'd have to convince him this is the best idea since sliced bread."

Dale was silent for a long moment. "Paul's not the only one with contacts."

"What do you mean?"

"I've got an online gardening chat group, connected with the church." He shrugged. "A lot of the people who are on it are parents, including Martha."

"Who's Martha?"

He smiled. "Martha *Wells*. Kyle's mum."

At first, they giggled, pulling faces at each other whenever their parents' backs were turned and even started moulding rude shapes out of the clay. Of course, they'd never done that in the original craft sessions in the church hall, not with Paul joining in. When I first saw one of them do it – a nine-year-old girl called Carly, her cheeks two pink spots of daring – I hesitated, my mouth dropped open until everyone was glancing at each other in silence, wondering what was wrong with me or if my internet had cut off.

Kyle leaned forward into his camera. "Elina? Are you still there?"

"Yes. Sorry, I just realised something. And I can see what you're doing Carly, we all can... But I just realised, this 'fight' you have inside of you. It's there all the time, so instinctive that you don't even notice it. You want to push against authority, I get that. You want to push the boundaries wherever you go; you're always testing to see what you can and can't get away with..."

Six pairs of eyebrows raised. Uncertain faces stared at their screens, at me and each other. *What was the crazy lady on about now? Did she really think she could be on our side – a grown-up?*

I leaned closer to my laptop. "Listen. I want you to apply the same thinking to your secret fears and worries. We all get scared sometimes. Yes, even me. *Especially* me. Sometimes I think adults get even more scared than kids do." Snuffling sounds as the shy ones covered their mouths, and Carly let out a cackle. "That's right. You might be braver than an adult. But I want you to *do* something with that. I want you to use it – no, not laugh at it, Carly. This is a talent you have, a special ability. Be a dare-devil. Stare back at fear and stick your tongue out."

They went quiet. Some of them (including Carly) actually stuck their tongues out, and I had to bite my own not to say, 'Not *now*.' It was okay; they could use this. I couldn't see their auras through the screens, but if there were colours to denote this cheeky, bubbling energy they had, I was sure they'd be glowing bright.

Soon they were channelling that energy into clay models, their small, determined fingers pushing into the clay and scooping out fearsome faces, pencil-end stares and sloping wings that would spread in the other plane – not that these kids would ever know it. I got them to make two each; one to give away, 'to guard the neighbourhood' as I called it, treating it like a war effort, and another one for themselves, presuming they'd want to keep some of their handiwork. If nothing else, the figurines would be reminders of an attitude they could always turn to, even if on a material level they ended up as doorstops or paperweights. It was worth the exercise just for that.

I wasn't worried about 'intriguing' the children into another world of horrors they couldn't handle: they already lived in it. They saw what I saw, but without the ability to fly further in and meet more of the same. All Dale and I needed was get a sense of who the children were, of their personal gripes and frustrations; then we'd have something to latch on to. But more than anything, it was their fight-back I wanted.

All that time I'd been looking at Kyle's gargoyle the wrong way. All I could see was how, inside that gargoyle, I kept getting swiped at, injured, pulled. It was my terror that kept drawing Fear towards me; the vulnerability which gargoyle represented was both a doorway and a trap. But the gargoyle kept going back for more; it wanted to be there, even when its wing was broken. It wanted to face down those things. That was more important and more powerful than any image I'd had in mind about Kyle's vulnerability; false ideas I'd built up over time because of his difficult home life. Well, thanks to Paul's intervention over the last year, Kyle's difficulties were mostly behind him – and, in a way, thanks to all the rotten treatment he'd got from his father, Kyle had grown into a strong, feisty, spirited person who wasn't afraid of Fear.

Of course, powerlessness never quite goes away. Our defence was just the same as anyone else's, just a belief, mixed with the force of intention. These kids had more than enough of it, and they could use it at ground level as their emotional armour. The rest they let go, let fly, like night terrors they didn't need to believe in any more. Afterwards, they'd skip off, ready do something else, not knowing why they felt that little bit lighter. It was our empathy – Dale's and mine – which gave their fight-back flight and unleashed all that energy on another level. Literally.

I felt bad about pulling the wool over Paul's eyes, but then I knew it wouldn't last: sooner or later he would find us in those skies, testing out our fleet. In the meantime, he could hardly argue with my decision to sit out and work on my meditation skills until I got a better hold on my anxieties, although he seemed surprised and a little edgy about me doing so in Dale's back garden.

I turned away when I saw the strain in his eyes. He was obviously worried about the Watchers being so few against the ever-swelling hordes of Fear-beasts. But that was the reason we had to try.

I couldn't risk Paul stopping us from trying. I owed Paul – and the others – and the rest of humanity, if I let myself think about it for more than a few seconds. My weakness was the reason the membrane had 'popped' another hole and why there were more goblins on this plane, at least locally.

I slipped out to Dale's in the late afternoon, into the green, tree-lined space that had become a haven to me over the past couple of days. I'd just got off the phone from Sarah who had to admit I was looking less fragile and more myself; she thoroughly approved of the online clay modelling sessions and had cheerfully 'threatened' to join in on one.

But I had to end the call quickly, fearing I couldn't keep up my light-hearted tone for much longer. The time had come to test out our fleet.

Dale had lined up all the gargoyles he'd collected from the children's houses, and we spent a little time considering each one and the personality of the child who'd made it: Carly with her non-stop cheekiness; Tanya with her solemn, deep-thinking stare, whose deep-eyed gargoyle had a bit of ghoulishness about it; Sunil's hesitant confidence and the wonky, stubby-headed but determined-looking beast of a clay model, with the fattest tongue of all. Kyle's original gargoyle stood among them, an unwitting, seasoned warrior, since Dale had superglued its broken wing back together.

Wrapped in our jackets against the cool air, we each settled our cushions against a tree and closed our eyes.

Dale didn't need to teach me how to split my attention multiple ways so I could fly in three of the gargoyles. By now I had several new terrors and hopes to match them – as if each emotion had an underside to it, an aura that stretched out like a thick ribbon, turning slowly in the air. It reminded me of when I flew to Dale's inside Sibelius, so livid the streets seemed lit up with quivering colours. Each new fear gave me an incentive to fight back; that's how I saw it now. I had no choice but to see it that way, because the alternative was just to lie down and let hopelessness wash over me.

One by one, our gargoyles flapped into the other plane. I even gave some thought to Sibelius so he could join in, sensing his chuckling at the sheer cheek of our rogue experiment.

Up I/we rose on the wings of acceptance, and empathy, and shared-ness with Dale's experiences. This guy whom I'd been so furious with just a short time ago; now I could only see how much we were the same. We felt so many things, all at once. And that didn't have to be a weakness. Not if we accepted what we were, and did something with it.

The clouds gathered closer around us, threatening to smother us, but all I felt was fire, determination. A bright new '*Hii-YA!*' like Kyle's martial arts arm-chop. Incredibly, unbelievably, the goblins' heads peeked nervously from their hiding places and winced back at the sight of us. As we got close, some of them actually shrank in size. Two disappeared completely as Carly's gargoyle showed its tongue, and her unique, glittering gold blew its cloud breath into the sky. There was something about our clay gargoyles that disturbed Fear and made those creatures nervous.

Inevitably, there was also a murder of crows up there who were almost as disturbed by our fleet as those goblins were.

Back on the ground I had some explaining to do.

Paul stood in Dale's back garden, frowning over his face mask, his eyes lit with disbelief.

"But, Paul, maybe the 'problems' of the second-generation Watchers aren't actually problems. What if we just can't quite follow the same rules as you? We can't all be so… neat and tidy. I've tried, and I can't leave all my grief and fear behind when I go up to that other plane."

I tapped my chest, remembering how I tried. "My fear comes with me, and I'm not sure I'll ever be able to change that. But you know better than anyone, that life isn't as simple as one side versus the other. You said yourself that Fear can never be destroyed, it's a part of life. Well, maybe it's all more entangled than we thought.

Like what Dale told me. His love for Kate is also pain and fear."

I'd watched astonishment quiver over Paul's face, one layer of it after another, but he didn't interrupt me until I stopped to take a breath. Was he going to chide me for our wild experiment? For breaking all the rules, and not even telling him? But he knew I knew too much, that Dale had filled me in on the history. The original Watchers hadn't known what they were doing either and had made mistakes along the way. If they really wanted our help, they had to allow the same of us.

"So..." He shook his head. "What are you saying?"

I sighed with gratefulness, and relief. "That we're a muddle, but that's okay. We'll face those things as the muddle that we are – and *split up* to spread ourselves further. All we need is a little imagination. And what we don't have, we can borrow."

Fear was everywhere, it was true; but there was nowhere *we* wouldn't go.

The children told their friends about the online clay modelling class, so it wasn't long before Dale and I held another. Our fleet grew. The crows gave us a wide berth at first, but seeing Sibelius in our midst, this didn't last long.

We were Watchers, scaring off the swathe of dread and anxiety fed by millions of fretting minds. We were a bit ghoulish, and more than a little makeshift, but what came out of us was the same thing as the crow-hosted spiritual teachers: love.

At last, I understood love. It's so much simpler than what I'd thought. It's what you give to other people. There's always more of it to give, because it's the natural result of how you see the world when you realise there are no limits, and no true boundaries between us.

While I was up there, inspiration called to me from the other side of the membrane. I began to feel its shape stirring inside me once more, the hints of artistic ideas that I might sculpt or paint. But I kept a respectful distance, my mind focussed on the job at hand. I remembered what I've always sort of known, instinctively; that inspiration flows best from invisible spaces and it thrives on mystery, on things not quite understood. It is a process of finding out, and I wanted to take my time with that journey.

I think of my life before all this, only a few days ago, and it's so different. It's like staring across a lake to the other side; to another me, a foreign shore, bleak and obscured by mist. Back then, all I could see was how I was failing, and falling. Believing in nothing, I had nothing to do except survive; my only true calling, my art and my sculpting, had been taken away from me – that's how I saw it. But all I had to think about was me. I didn't understand that I was a part of everything, and everyone. I was busy staring at my empty hands when right above me was the wide-open sky.

I held four online crafting sessions in the end; well, three and a half. I began to feel unwell in the fourth one, so I handed over to Kyle. He's hosted another one since on his own; being so young, technology comes naturally to him. He's my chief gargoyle maker, master Fear-sneerer and head teacher of the craft. He hardly knows all the things he's capable of, but I think he's beginning to see it. Sometimes life tests us, and we push back, discovering muscles we didn't think we had.

I got tested for coronavirus, and it came back positive; just like it did for Jake, our trainer at work. Our manager, Clare, rang to tell me soon after my result came through, so I told her my news in the same call.

I suppose it was shock, but Clare sounded false, like a voiceover for an advert as she apologised and asked me about where I was living. "Are you going to be okay?" she said, presumably meaning my home circumstances or whether I'd stocked enough toilet roll or bread. The silence that followed swelled with awkwardness before she backtracked over her faux pas, stuttering another apology.

Is anyone going to be okay? We don't know. We never know. It's just that some circumstances highlight this uncertainty more sharply than others.

But I've changed. In a weird way, I'm glad life threw me down this sudden fork in the road. I started off just like those kids, believing I had no power; that life had taken it away from me. But even when you are stripped bare of everything you have, when your ambitions are a million miles away and you don't even know if you might die soon, you still have that light you can shine. The power you have is in your own reaction. So long as you are breathing, you can choose how to think about it all, how to respond. I stick my tongue out at anxiety, and I help others do the same.

And as for Fear, and as for death, and all the unconquerable things that we are stuck with in this life…

I don't know why we have to fight, but that's all we can do: fight for each other, with love, with every scrap of hope we can muster.

And if I could believe there's a higher purpose to it all – and sometimes, when I lie awake after flying in that other plane, I wonder if maybe I do – it would be this: it makes us realise what we are and what we're capable of.

Be strong. Stay safe.

Backword

There's a reason why books are shaped like doors; you open them up and they take you somewhere else. The mind is a strange place and what's inside yours might also be inside someone else's, or may overlap into another place entirely. The only way to know for sure is to read, imagine, and follow the secrets that unfold in Anna Tizard's Deeply Weird newsletter by subscribing at: www.annatizard.com. You'll receive updates, anecdotes and other exclusive material not published anywhere else!

Thank you for reading *The Empty Danger*. I hope you enjoyed it! I'd be enormously grateful if you could leave an honest review on your book seller's platform and also on Goodreads too, if you use it. Help others make the same discovery!

About the Author

Anna Tizard's *deeply weird* fiction explores the strangeness of the human mind and imagines what it might what happen if our thoughts were places, creatures or objects come alive. Her influences include Neil Gaiman, Philip Pullman and the theories of Carl Jung. Anna studied English Literature at Cardiff University and now lives in Brighton, UK.

Printed in Great Britain
by Amazon